THE OFFICIAL NOVELIZATION

CHRISTIAN FRANCIS

BASED ON THE SCREENPLAY BY MICHAEL NANKIN

 ECHO ON PUBLICATIONS

echohorror.com

CONTENTS

Foreword

by Michael Nankin

It isn't often a filmmaker gets an opportunity to revisit a project 40 years after it's release. Many of us don't even live that long. I wrote *The Gate* during a dark period of my life and I found comfort dredging up all my childhood friends and fears and translating them through the dark glass of my depression. I was 30 years old and had given up everything in Los Angeles to move to New York and make a film – a project which collapsed and left me broke and living with my parents. I was facing what seemed like a bleak future as a Hollywood's youngest has-been. I knew I had to reinvent myself and so I re-read *The Necronomicon* and a ton of other horror novels and wrote *The Gate* in a 4-week sprint of late nights and restless dreams. I even started hearing voices at 3am, one of which asked me, "Do you want to see something?" Electrified with fear, I replied with an emphatic "No!" and turned on all the lights. During the day, I wonder if I made the right choice. At night, I'm certain that I did.

So I sold the script and the move got made and I was back in business. It became the highest-grossing Canadian produced film ever and outperformed the presumed blockbuster released the same weekend, *Ishtar*. Every newspaper carried the story of the $40 million Goliath bested by the $3 million David. "You see, all it takes is a good idea" most of the reviews concluded -- and I was a hero. Only it wasn't quite the movie I wanted. Much of the darkness had been scrubbed out and, because the protagonists were children, the movie catered to children. Not quite the subversive message I was after.

So, 40 years later, enter the lovely Christian Francis who read all my early drafts and created a version familiar to fans of the movie, yet resurrected much of my prankster boy nastiness and presents this delightful souffle of dark and light. So turn the lights low, wait until 3 in the morning and crack open this ancient tome.

You want to see something?

CHAPTER 1

MOTHS

Twisted, strange voices echoed throughout the tunnels deep, deep under the ground. These circular passages had not been excavated by any machine but instead clawed through, mud and filth gouged by talons and teeth. Claustrophobic and tight, each of these ancient, labyrinthine corridors snaked through the earth, intersecting in what made up a complex maze.

The voices came from above and were so muffled and indiscernible it almost sounded as if they were some distant instruments, playing low, bassy notes that mumbled down into the tunnels.

Through the subterranean blackness, a scaled hand with three gnarled claws dug into the earth, pulling its cadaverous, gaunt body along, frantically chasing the source of the sound. Its other clawed hand then did the same as its feet propelled it through the narrow passages. Dirt rubbed against its thick, leathery skin as it scrambled upward.

This creature exhaled in ragged growls; each one with guttural menace. Coming to a stop every so often, it paused to hear the voices again to check the direction it was clawing toward.

Farther and farther, it traveled, both upward and downward, round the tightest of corners and through the tiniest of crevices leading to other parallel passages. It was a dizzying, relentless journey as it hunted the sounds as if it were a smell from their prey.

Above, the tunnels it scrambled through soon opened up, wider and higher, allowing the creature to scurry faster. No longer pulling itself through a narrow catacomb, it could break into a scurry, picking up speed in the hunt of whatever made these sounds. Above, thin roots soon began to poke their way out the dirt ceiling as the surface world above came nearer and nearer.

The creature's breathing became more stilted and frantic as it started to smell the world above it. The odors of life that seeped down through the soil.

As it turned a corner, this thing immediately came to a stop, instantly frozen as it saw something. Something that its black eyes could see clearly despite the absence of light down in this maze. Just ahead, a small bundle of fur wrapped around living meat sat in the middle of this creature's path, having dug through from a nearby burrow.

This critter turned, alerted to the creature that stared hungrily at it. This hapless animal did not know it had ventured into somewhere so dangerous. It did not understand what happened as it opened its toothy mouth and squealed painfully, then began convulsing on the dirt beneath. With terrifying speed, this animal's fur began to wither as its flesh collapsed inwards. Its skin quickly dried as it pulled back in a horrific decay.

The animal screeched in torment as the creature watched on coldly. Its gnarled claws twitched as it basked in this interloper's agony, releasing a gleeful moan from its reptile-like lips.

As the creature lingered on this new kill, the voices above grew louder, joined by a rising whirring sound. One that quickly became a cacophonous roar of shrieking metal on cracking wood. One that shook the very earth itself.

In reply, the creature shrieked as if trying to ward off the deafening sounds above it. Soon the shrieks from one became many as farther down the infinite tunnel complex, more and more creatures joined in on the rage.

"That's it, whoa!" the workman shouted as the circular saw cutting the thick branches off the old, gnarled tree, came to a whining stop.

The noise of the spinning metal against splintering

wood was soon replaced by the ambient sound of the suburbs on an autumn day.

By the end of August, the heatwave had abandoned Toronto, leaving behind a lingering sun illuminated with a deceptive brightness. In its place, a crisp chill filled into the air, in what was a sharp prelude to winter. This particular morning was no exception. The sun hung impotently in the sky; its rays powerless to warm as the backyard grass glistened with a layer of dew. And for these workmen, they had to wear many layers to ward off the bite in the air.

A dozen thick ropes were wrapped around the stripped tree trunk, leading to a bulldozer on the other side of the Simon's backyard. The men stood around to watch as the machine lurched forward and, with all its might, ripped the large, dead tree from out of the earth. Its expansive, rotten roots exposed to the daylight for the first time.

As the tree came crashing down onto the lawn, the rickety treehouse that had been stuck in the middle of its decrepit branches cracked apart. The rope swing that had hung on the branches for many years now lay on the grass.

There was no waiting or delaying, as all the men quickly picked up their chainsaws and began to cut into the felled trunk.

In one of the bedrooms of the Simon's house, ten-year-old Glen Simon lay on his bed, staring at the ceiling. Having been woken by the buzzing saw, he had stayed under the covers as the noise from the backyard washed over him. So too did the feeling of deep sadness. That treehouse was *his* and whether the tree was deemed dangerous to climb was beside the point. He did not want it cut down. He did not want his treehouse stolen away from him without even a consultation. Yet he had no say in any of this.

He hadn't had the nerve to watch as the tree fell, but he had heard it. Sounding like a final scream for help. It was only when the chainsaws stopped that Glen decided to get out of bed and look out of the window at what had been done.

From where the roots had been pulled up, they had taken with them a large amount of the ground, leaving a big pit in the earth, a pit a few of the workmen looked into. The tree itself lay in pieces on the grass, seeming to Glen like a crime scene from a television show as a victim lay, cold and breathless, and detectives milled around looking for evidence.

But there was no use feeling sad anymore. What was done was done. His treehouse was gone. There was no bringing it back. At least his father agreed to keep the wood in case a new one could be built somewhere. With a resigned sigh, Glen threw a jacket on over his pajamas and decided to go visit the crime scene for himself.

"Jesus," one of the workmen said as he stared at the

tree's crumbling roots. "This thing's rotted from the bottom up!"

Another workman, carrying a chunk of trunk to a wheelbarrow, nodded. "Even the friggin' termites are dead on this thing."

Glen stood and watched as the tree was carted away, piece by piece, until all that was left was smatterings of sawdust across the grass, a pile of treehouse planks, and the large exposed hole in the ground.

Staring into this pit, Glen's mind raced.

"Cool out, dude. They'll never know," Terry said with a mischievous grin to Glen, who was out of his pajamas and dressed in jeans and a T-shirt under a jacket.

Terry Chandler, a year older than Glen, yet in the same grade at school, was a small wiry child. With thick glasses in dark plastic frames, he almost always wore the same denim jacket, littered in sewn-on patches from various heavy metal bands.

Terry stood in the new hole in the backyard and was ready to dig some more. Having already moved the excavated grass and left it rolled up a few feet away, these boys had dug up what the workmen had previously filled in.

"You can't back out now," Terry said. "It was *your* idea!"

"I know it was," Glen sighed as he turned to look

at the house. "But I told my dad, and he said we should leave it alone."

From the porch, staring back at him, was Angus. A fifteen-year-old golden retriever who had seen better days. A dog who spent most of his days sleeping or moving achingly slowly about the house.

"Well, that's on him," Terry scoffed. "Just because he didn't believe you." He turned his gaze back down to the dirt at his feet. "I bet you're right. There's all kinds of minerals and stuff down there. There could be gold, anything!"

"Yeah, I—"

"And he won't be mad if we *do* find something, will he?"

Terry was going to do this no matter what. He was invested in this after Glen had suggested a treasure hunt. "Besides, we'll fill it right back in after! What harm can it do anyone, huh?"

"Yeah," Glen said with a smile. "Suppose you're right. We could find anything down there. We *have* to look!" Shaking off his doubt, he picked up the old shovel from the grass and tossed it over to Terry.

Catching it one-handed, Terry winced as a splinter on the handle cut into the flesh of his index finger. "Jiminy goddamn Cricket!" He yelped through gritted teeth as a rivulet of blood dribbled out from the small wound and fell down to the dirt at his feet.

"Oh god, I'm so sorry!" Glen almost shouted with a guilty look.

With his finger stuck in his mouth, Terry sucked

the blood and chuckled. "Sorry? Why? You do that on purpose, eh, Mr. Simon? You out to kill me?"

On the porch, Angus stared at the boys and let out a quiet, scared whine. Watching them digging made Angus nervous, but he did not know why.

The afternoon wind kicked up leaves around them as Terry looked at his finger. The cut was deeper than he thought. At least the bleeding had stopped. Shrugging it off, he picked up the shovel.

"You should put some Bactine on that," Glen suggested. "Could get infected, then your finger will fall off. Then your hand."

"Anything else?"

Glen shrugged. "Maybe your butt next?"

Terry let out a loud laugh as he lifted the shovel and slammed it down into the earth. As it did, the shovel jarred against something solid, sending a judder through him, making him let out a shocked gasp.

"You are kiddin' me?" he exclaimed. "I hit a rock? Already?"

Glen got into the hole and knelt next to him. With his hands, he dug at the solid lump that the shovel collided with. "This is cool," he muttered as the rock's surface glittered with the dirt brushed away.

About the size of a loaf of bread, the rock had a large gash across it, the shovel's tip having cut into it.

"Is that . . . ?" Terry asked as he crouched beside Glen, holding the strange-looking rock. His face lit up. "It is! It's a geode!"

"A who-what now?"

Terry was immediately on his feet again, shovel in hand, ready to keep digging. "I bet there's more down there," he said as he slammed the shovel into the dirt a second time. But instead of hitting any more rock, the shovel slid out of his hands as it broke through the earth and fell into a space below. As it did, a large plume of brown smoke billowed up through the hole in to their aces.

"Peeyeeeew!" Glen whined, holding his nose from the rank smell the cloud had carried with it.

Terry's face contorted as the smell hit him, too. "Oh, jeez, that smells of Angus's farts!"

"Did something die down there?" Glen said, almost tasting the smell.

"Only one way to find out."

Before Glen could stop him, Terry was on all fours and threw his hand into the hole beneath. "What are you doin'? That's a really bad idea. You could fall in."

But Terry plunged on. The small opening widened quickly as he jammed his hand through the hole. The dirt crumbled and fell in around the edges as he fished around in the dark for more treasure.

"There could be anything!" Terry said excitedly as his imagination ran rampant. "Diamonds, rubies. Hell, this could be one of those Indian graves . . . They could have buried the geode with them. We could find a skeleton!"

"I don't think they're graves down there," Glen

said, more trying to convince himself. "It's too small to be a grave, right?"

Terry was shoulder-deep. His happy expression of wonder abruptly dropped as his hand brushed against something strange. Pausing, he summoned all his bravery and grabbed hold of whatever it was, pulling it out of the hole.

As the sunlight shone down on them, Terry and Glen were there at the hole, staring at the desiccated remains of a small gopher.

With a mutual yelp, Terry dropped the dead animal. Its husk of a body tumbled down, back into the pit below.

"I guess that explains the smell," Glen said, fighting back a rising feeling of losing his lunch. He then realized that Terry had picked up the animal with his cut finger. "You're gonna need more than Bactine for that."

Terry looked at his finger in horror, then at Glen. "I don't want my butt to fall off," he said before bursting into laughter again.

Before they could say any more, a sudden fluttering sound drifted out of the hole, up toward them. A soft, papery sound, that was building in volume. Like dozens of tiny wings. *Hundreds.* Getting closer.

"We should fill this in now," Glen said in a slight panic, motioning to the shovel. "*Right now.*"

As if on cue, a swarm of moths flew out of the hole and filled the air around the boys, flying in cyclonic movements. The sun caught on their pale wings before they turned and flitted off into the sky. Leaving both boys staring at each other, amazed and bewildered.

"Wow," Glen said. "What the hell was that?"

"I bet they lived in the tree, probably dug underground for winter," Terry said, clearly having no idea what he was talking about. "Then again, you know this house *is* a grave site, right?"

"Aw, shut up. It is not!" Glen shot back. "There's no Indians."

Terry smiled as he spoke. Letting rip a flight of fancy. "No, not Indians, worse. Americans! I heard that, when they were building this house, they used a firm from Chicago. And one of the builders got killed, right? The rest of the crew were afraid to call the police, 'cause they were not from 'round here, so they sealed the body up inside one of the walls in there."

"And that has exactly *what* to do with a hole in the ground full of moths?"

"Who knows? Maybe the dead worker infected the ground with his fury at not being properly buried? Maybe all this ground is now poisoned with his death. And you know moths love death?" Terry then shrugged. "Anyways, just saying what I heard."

With a smirk, Glen turned his gaze back to the geode lying on the dirt beside them. "And what about that?" He laughed. "That's the murder weapon, right?"

As Terry was about to reply, they were interrupted

by the sound of crashing metal coming from behind them.

Turning, they saw Al, Alexandra Simon, Glen's fifteen-year-old sister, standing at the side of the house. She was dumping heavy contents from a cardboard box into one of the trash cans. She was dressed like an *Into the Groove*-era Madonna from Goodwill.

Glen's expression fell as he realized what his sister was throwing away. "Al," he called out. "Don't! Wait a sec!"

Both he and Terry raced over the lawn, to where she stood, staring back at them, the empty box dangling from her hand.

"What are you doing?" Glen asked, panting from his sudden burst of movement.

"Me?" Al replied, staring at the hole in the ground. "What are *you* doing? Didn't Dad say you couldn't dig?"

"But there could be treasure," Glen replied, honestly believing in his plan.

Terry, meanwhile, stared at what Al had thrown out: model rocket paraphernalia, cardboard tubes, old batteries, and finger-sized rocket engines.

Glen continued. "And you can't throw this stuff away, you just can't." He motioned to the trash can as a look of genuine hurt crept over his face. "You said I could help you launch them."

"Yeah, well," Al shrugged. "That was then. I'm not gonna launch 'em now."

"But you *promised*."

Al looked at her brother, then at Terry, who was still staring at the trash can as if it were pirate treasure. She rolled her eyes. "Look, if I *were* launching 'em, you could help. But I'm not. I'm throwing them away. You can help me do that instead."

Glen was deflated. "But, Al," he whined.

"Alexandra," she corrected sternly. "I told you to stop calling me Al. I'm not Al."

Glen stared at the discarded rocket materials forlornly. "Why don't you just let me have this stuff? You don't have to chuck it all away, you know?"

Al sighed. She was tired of this conversation. "'Cause Mom and Dad said it was too dangerous for you to do any of this unsupervised."

"Then, supervise me!" Glen insisted.

Before he could try any more to convince her, a car horn honked from the front of the house. Al glanced over her shoulder with a smile. Turning back to her brother, she then excitedly thrust the cardboard box into his hands.

"Here, take this instead." She smiled, turning to leave. "Now, you guys don't get any ideas. And fill in that hole or dad's gonna kill you."

Glen would not relent. "But, what about Big Bertha?"

Stopping in her tracks, Al turned with a curious expression. "What are you talking about? What do *you* know about Big Bertha?"

Glen smiled, knowing he could force this situation. "Oh, I know *all* about it."

The car horn honked again impatiently. But Al, despite being in a rush, had to finish this conversation first.

"Like what? Exactly?" she inquired, sternly. Hushed.

Glen could barely hide his glee. "I know that you swiped it on the Fourth of July from the stand. And I know it's illegal for you to have. And I know you could burn down the whole neighborhood with it if you wanted. You'd be in so much trouble if anyone found out!"

With an exasperated sigh, Al stepped closer, her voice almost a whisper, not wanting anyone to overhear. "Well, for your information, Big Bertha is gone. I got rid of that thing. It's gone forever, okay?"

Glen's glee fell to disappointment. "Oh," he said, taken aback.

The car horn honked again with even greater impatience. Then again. And again.

"Well, sayonara, losers," Al said with a smile. "I gotta go." She hurried around the front of the house, leaving them standing by the trash cans. "And don't touch those damn rockets," she called out loudly as she disappeared from sight.

"Where's she going?" Terry asked.

"Patty and Stacy's probably."

"Patty and Stacy?" Terry wrinkled his nose in

disgust as he thought of them. "The gross Lee sisters?"

Turning to each other, they both made the same gagging sound before bursting out in fits of laughter.

"The question is," Terry said, "are these the same moths?"

He was staring at the fence in the backyard, at a pale moth that sat upon it. In his hand, he held a glass jar. A jar that contained five other identical moths.

"They're just minding their own business," Glen said, his attention on other things a few meters away.

"This little guy could have seen so many things down there. Could have met the mole people, flown round all the forgotten underground cities." With an almost expert precision, Terry then raised his hand and grabbed the moth before it could flutter away.

It fluttered between his grip in a blind panic.

"Aw, leave 'em alone," Glen complained, looking over to what Terry was doing. "That could hurt 'em."

Terry quickly deposited his new catch in with the other moths and shut the lid tight. "You ever seen so many in one place before?"

Sitting across the lawn, nearer to the hole, Glen had no care for any of the moths. He was too busy, kneeling in front of the newly built rocket launching pad made from the cut-up cardboard box and using bits Al threw away. In his hand, he held a half assembled eighteen-inch rocket.

"Why did she have to throw it all away?" Glen mused, looking at all the parts spread out on the cardboard in front of him.

Terry walked over and sat beside him. "Why did she? That's an easy one. The Lee sisters are tryin' to turn her into a girl. See how she's dressing now? Like a Kmart Barbie. That's what my mom calls that look." He lifted the jar of moths to his face and shook it. Forcing the moths to dart about their glass confines in a frenzy. He looked at them, entranced. "How long do you think they can keep flying for?"

Glen was too engaged in the rockets to answer.

"Astronauts!" Terry said excitedly. "Let's fly the moths up into space."

"Would if we could but look?" He motioned to all the rocket parts. "It's all junk. All these bits are totaled. Can't find one bit that'll work."

"Oh," Terry replied, disappointed.

"Guess I gotta put 'em all back in the trash," Glen moaned.

Terry shook the moth jar again. "We should do an experiment, anyway." He then quickly unscrewed the jar, fished his hand in, and grabbed a moth out from within, careful to not let the others escape. Screwing the lid back on, he then stared wide-eyed at the creature clamped between his fingers. "They are so gross-looking close up."

Glen did not like that Terry put them in a jar and wanted him to just set them free.

"I just want to see if this works," Terry said as he

reached up and grabbed one of the moth's tiny legs, which was trying to kick out in fear.

Glen went pale as he realized what his friend was about to do. "Don't—" He winced as he heard the soft ripping sound.

Its curled proboscis quivered as its unblinking, alien-like eyes stared in horror. The moth was trying all it could to escape as Terry ripped off each of its legs, one by one.

Glen sat there, not believing his friend could be so cruel to anything.

"It's not just the hole and the rockets," Michael Simon said angrily as he sat at the kitchen table alongside Glen, Al, and his wife Marcy.

With a meatloaf plated in front of them, the family were in the middle of dinner. And from the conversation, it had been a tense one for Glen, as his father spoke sternly, peering over his glasses as he lectured. "It's a matter of irresponsibility, you know? And all this the night before we leave. It really makes me wonder whether you two can be trusted in this house all alone. I mean, what would we come back to? The whole yard a dig site? The house burned to the ground?"

Al looked annoyed at her brother, then turned to her father with a pleading expression. "Oh, Daddy, you promised me!" she said in her most innocent tone. "I'm old enough to take care of him. You *know* I am. I swear, there won't be any trouble while you're gone. None."

Glen looked ashamed as he focused on the plate of food in front of him.

Below him, hidden under the tablecloth, Angus sat, staring. Resting his head upon Glen's knee. Quietly begging for scraps.

Grabbing a chunk of meatloaf from off his plate, Glen handed it slyly to Angus, who happily swallowed it without even chewing.

Glen's mom, Marcy, smiled as she noticed.

"I just don't know," Michael continued in his most parental tone. "It's not too late to call Mrs. Vandegrift to babysit. She said she could if we needed her."

Al's face dropped. "Oh, please! You *can't* call her. You said I was mature enough to be responsible. I promise, there really, really won't be any trouble."

Michael glanced at Marcy, who gave him a knowing wink in return. They had no intention of calling in a babysitter. This was all just the charade they needed to do as parents. He then turned to Glen, who was playing with his food, moving the meatloaf remnants around his plate with a fork.

"Well, what do you think?" his dad asked. "*Can* you be trusted?"

Glen shrugged, not looking up. "I don't know." When he finally glanced up, he saw his sister staring daggers back at him, and his maudlin demeanor immediately lifted as he realized the implications of this conversation. "I mean . . . yes," he corrected, turning to his dad. "I can be trusted."

"If . . ." Marcy added, jumping into the parental fray. "And I mean IF your father, and I agree to let you two stay alone for three whole days, how can we be *sure* that you'll behave? And not do something silly, like dig up the backyard?"

"It wasn't me, though," Glen protested. "Terry started it."

Marcy shook her head. "And I suppose if Terry jumped off a bridge, you'd jump off too?"

Glen looked at her, confused. "Why would he jump off a bridge?"

"Mom, Dad," Al interrupted. "I can handle Terry, and I can handle Glen, and I can handle the house. Please trust me. You can think what you want about Glen, but you know you can leave me in charge. You know I'm sensible."

With a smile, Michael glanced at Marcy before speaking. "All right," he said, wiping his mouth with a napkin. "We are going to trust you. But if you let us down, you'll be babysat by Mrs. Vandegrift until you're both eighteen years old. Understand me?"

Al smiled as she relaxed back into her chair. "Absolutely."

"But as for you, young man," Michael said to Glen, "you are grounded for the weekend, and that means that you don't leave this house until we get back."

"Grounded?" Glen said, dumbfounded. "For a hole?"

"And it starts tonight, right after you fill it in back to how it was."

"I told you not to play with the rockets," Al said snidely, holding a flashlight beam at Glen as he busily filled in the hole in the backyard. "I saw they were gone from the trash."

The backyard was pitch black save for the moonlight and the flashlight. No streetlamps managed to cast their glow this far behind the house.

Lifting a clump of dirt onto his shovel, Glen quickly dropped it into the nearly filled hole. "Remember a long time ago, when you got two of the same rockets for your birthday, and we took 'em down to the wash? We tied 'em together, and they went really high, higher than any other rocket we'd seen?"

"And?"

"And that was loads of fun, right?" He spoke as he lifted another shovel of earth and threw it into the hole.

"Sure, I guess."

"It was fun, Al," Glen said as he started to pack down the dirt with the back side of his shovel.

"It's *Alexandra*. How many times do I have to tell you that?" She shook her head in annoyance.

"Anyway, aren't you done yet? My hair's starting to frizz out here."

Glen looked horrified. "Frizzing? Who *are* you?"

Al shot him a look of annoyance.

Glen sighed. "I'll finish this myself. You can just go in . . . *Alexandra*."

"Fine," she replied, placing the flashlight on the grass and pointing the beam at him. Without another word, she walked back toward the house.

"Fine," Glen repeated to himself with a hurt pout. He turned back to the hole, scraping the last bits of dirt from the grass beside it.

With a sudden, loud pop, the bulb in the flashlight shattered, plunging Glen into immediate darkness. On the next beat, the shovel in his hand emitted a loud cracking noise.

Unable to see much, Glen could only stand in the murky darkness in quiet shock, wondering what had happened. He felt down at the wooden handle of the spade and felt the splintered wood, where the metal head had somehow now snapped off.

"Al," he muttered in a weak, fearful tone, but she was already gone.

Not wanting to stay out here a second longer and not understanding what could have just happened to the flashlight or shovel, Glen bolted back toward the safety of his house.

. . .

Lying in bed, ready to sleep, the covers pulled up to his nose, Glen could not shake what happened in the backyard. The lights in his bedroom were still on as his father opened the door and leaned in.

"Good night, buddy," he said with a smile as he reached for the light switch.

"Please," Glen quickly said, worried. "Leave it on."

With a flash of concern, Michael pulled his hand back and walked in. "What's with you today?" he asked, sitting down on the side of the bed. "You're digging up the backyard, disobeying me after I said that you couldn't. Then you ran in, now afraid of the dark? You've never been like that before."

"I don't know," Glen replied quietly. "It's something . . . it's . . . since we dug the hole."

"Well, you filled it in, didn't you? Are you afraid of something in there or something?"

Glen swallowed. "Well, yeah, but . . . Terry told me something."

Terry, Michael thought. *It's always Terry. That kid's gonna end up in jail someday.*

"What did Terry tell you?" Michael asked, hiding his true feelings about Glen's best friend.

"I thought he was joking. But he said a person died as they were building the house. And the others buried his body in the walls so they wouldn't get blamed. And the ground is poisoned or something with his . . ." Glen's mind raced, trying to piece everything together. "I dunno, but he somehow made the ground bad. And when Terry dug the hole . . . And the shovel snapped in half . . ."

Michael sighed. He sometimes forgot that his son was so young. That he was not even a teenager yet and was very impressionable. "This house is almost ninety years old. How could Terry possibly know what happened when they built it?"

Glen stared, wide-eyed, at his father, unable to answer the question.

Michael continued. "Let me tell you something about Terry, okay?" As he spoke, he kept a kind, calm tone. Choosing his words as carefully as he could. "You remember his mom went to heaven last year?"

Glen nodded.

"Well, ever since then, Terry's been a little . . . wild." I spoke to his dad about it. He likes . . . to live in a fantasy. To hide from the sadness. I think he's so sad his mom's gone that he makes stuff up sometimes." Michael smiled as he spoke. "He told his dad a few months back that he saw a pirate ship on the way home from school."

"He . . . he didn't?" Glen asked, sounding surprised.

"We don't live near any sea. Where would he have seen it?"

Something so obvious never occurred to Glen. Terry had told him that, too, and he had believed it. They even went to find it again over a weekend.

"He also has broken a few things at home. Smashed a plate, broke a window. All lashing out 'cause he's sad. So, just try to remember that if he gets destructive or tells you a story that is scary or unbelievable that he's just sad about his mom. You can be his friend, but it doesn't mean you have to believe all he says or do all he does, if it means you get in trouble. Do you know what I'm saying?"

Glen thought for a moment, then nodded. He had no idea that his friend was so sad. It was Terry. He had never seen him cry or be angry. He was just . . . . Terry. He knew so many stories about the town, and, sure, they got in trouble sometimes but . . . he felt bad that his friend was so sad that he did not know it.

"Good," Michael said as he leaned down and kissed Glen on the forehead. "Now, good night, Tiger."

As his father left, switching the light off and leaving the room in the hue of the moon, Glen stared at the ceiling. He stared at the shadows from the nearby trees silently snaking in and flitting across the plaster above him.

Pulling the sheets even tighter around his face, Glen looked around his bedroom, to the gloom coating all his posters and toys. Then, his gaze fell to the blank section of wall near his wardrobe.

Was Terry just making it up? He thought to himself. Did he just invent a story about a dead builder? If he did, why? What for?

Staring at the wall, he heard a flitting sound. It was not a surprise. Glen knew what it was. On the dresser by the door sat the jar of moths. Terry had taken glee in pulling the legs off them one at a time. Intent on seeing how long they could fly for. And they still flapped around their glass prison in a pained hysteria, unable to land, unable to rest. Terry had gotten bored with his experiment quite quickly and had intended to empty the jar over the fence. Glen, though, feeling bad for the moths, intervened and took the jar from him, saying he wanted to study them. He hated that Terry did this to the poor creatures. But he would never tell his friend that. He just let his friend believe he wanted to know the answer to his cruel question, too. But really, though, he just wanted to keep them inside. Warm. Not knowing if that is what they wanted or not. He had even put some drops of water in the bottom of the jar in case they wanted a drink as well as a couple of leaves in case that's what they ate. Instead, these moths just flew in circles, in a constant frenzy.

Yet he just stared at them pitifully keeping aloft. Their wings flapped desperately as their bodies thumped against the glass of the jar. But as this soft flapping sound continued, Glen drifted off to sleep.

CHAPTER 2

THE PARTY

The next morning, the chill in the air bit less than the day before, but for Glen, it was just as annoying. He missed the summer. He missed the warmth. He missed playing up in his treehouse. But the season, like his hideaway, had gone. Now all that was left was a pile of wood around the side of the house and the filled hole in the backyard.

His father had only just laid the grass over the dirt Glen had abandoned the night before. But even so, the hole did not appear as healthy as it should have. It was sunken slightly, and the once-green grass appeared to be graying.

The abandoned, broken flashlight and shovel had since been removed, and all that was left was this dying patch of sagging grass.

Glen dared not step on the grass itself, in fear of the ground giving way and him falling into whatever was below. Instead, he crouched as he looked and listened intently. Hoping he would not see or hear anything but expecting that another fluttering of moths or gust of that foul air could burst forth.

"Glen!" came his father's call. "We're off now!"

When Glen first found out that his parents were going away on a short holiday, he was sad. Normal kids would have been immediately ecstatic. Three days where he could do what he wanted? No supervision? No curfew? No rules? It sounded like a normal ten-year-old boy's dream. But this wasn't new. The only difference was that there was no babysitter hired to dictate their lives. Al was handed that responsibility for once. But still, his parents were going off for a few days without them. *Again.*

Glen had spoken about this to Terry, and naturally, his opinion was that Glen's parent had to be spies. Maybe these holidays were when they had to assassinate a politician, steal government secrets, or fly back to their own country for a new assignment. As to what country they spied for, Terry had guessed, *They don't look Russian, but that's the point, right? They're perfect spies. No one would guess Mr. and Mrs. Simon were, in fact, Mr. and Mrs. Simonski.*

Glen found this idea funny at the time, but every time his parents went away without him, he could not help but take it to heart.

As he walked through the side gate leading out front, Glen could see his parents sitting in the car happily. With the engine running, they were more than ready to leave, and from the impatient look on their faces, it couldn't come quick enough.

Al was leaning into the open driver's side window as her father, Michael, gave her the final instructions.

". . . And don't forget that Angus gets his pills every single day. Make sure that they're hidden in the dog food, or he'll spit them right back out again."

"And I don't want him on the furniture," Marcy added, already annoyed at the thought of finding dog hairs on her precious cushions.

"Yeah, I know, I know," Al replied obediently. "You told me all this already."

"Here is our itinerary." Michael handed her a sheet of paper. "The phone numbers we'll be at each day are listed at the top. If you need us for any emergency, don't be afraid to call. But *only* emergencies. Okay? Just be responsible."

Al nodded as Glen sidled up beside her.

"See you both in a few days," Marcy called out with a happy smile.

Glen attempted a smile back, but it came out as a thin-lipped grimace.

"Remember, you're grounded this weekend," Michael said to Glen.

With only a *We'll miss you both!* from their mother and a *No parties* warning from their father, the car quickly backed out of the drive at an eager speed.

As they waved their parents off, Al and Glen turned at each other with a similar despondent expression. Despite their differences, they both felt a slight tinge of abandonment. Right up until Al remembered her plans for the next few days and grinned widely.

"This is gonna be so rad," she said.

That evening, the strains of Madonna's latest single echoed throughout the house as Al's party was in full swing. A dozen fifteen- and sixteen-year-olds had taken over the living room. From what was a pristine room, where every magazine was at a ninety-degree angle to the edge of the tables and every photo frame was purposefully positioned on every shelf, to now, where half-eaten pizza boxes lay open, chips and chocolate in open packets. Each kid had also brought along stolen beer and liquor from their respective parent's houses, which they drank, each pretending they actually liked the tastes. The windows were also wide open, letting the smell of marijuana out and the evening air in. Everyone was too warm with alcohol to notice the chill. Despite all the booze and dope, it was quite a tame event. Just a bit on the messy side.

The only person not drinking or smoking was Al, who was making a concerted effort to keep things tidy while not appearing like a downer. No one noticed as she slipped coasters under drinks, picked up stray potato chips before they had a chance to be crushed into the carpet, or moved an ashtray closer to the window.

Eric Cleland, the oldest boy there, was someone

who considered himself a jock despite being terrible at most sports. Being a tall, well-built kid, he could carry off wearing a letterman style jacket to complete the look without anyone questioning it. With blonde hair and a handsome yet neanderthal face, he was one of the popular freshmen at Al's school. And also, one of the least intellectual. The sort of person who found it hilarious to show girls the food he was chewing by sticking out his tongue.

But he was not the center of attention at this party. That would be the identical twins who ran the ninth grade. They were the ones who brought their Madonna vinyls to provide the sole soundtrack to the party. No other music allowed. And they were also the ones who Al tried to copy with their style. With hair teased to the heavens, adorned with scrunchies and bows, ripped fishnets under a flouncy skirt, T-shirts slashed at the shoulders, and layers upon layers of mismatched costume jewelry, chunky beads, oversized crosses and stacks of bangles jangling on both wrists, heavily lined eyes, thick mascara and bright eyeshadow in electric blue and neon pink. They wore too much of . . . well, everything.

And in the living room, the sisters never stop talking.

They were the Lee sisters, Patty and Stacy.

Around them, Angus had been making a nuisance of himself, whining at the music, eating the dip, breathing his old dog breath on people as he tried to get their attention, just begging to be petted. Angus was by no means a bad dog, but he was an anxious one. He felt left out of everything as his humans went about their lives, rarely giving him any time. They used to play with him for hours, but it was only Glen who showed him any of the attention he so craved.

When he had trundled over to Patty and Stacy and they smelled something bad, they were not happy.

"Get that gross thing out of here. He just farted," they said in disgust, much to the amusement of Eric.

Angus may have not understood the words, but he understood the intention and the tone, and he lowered his tail sadly. He was led away from the party by Al, who gripped him by the collar and walked him upstairs.

"Here," Al said, leading the dog into Glen's room "Take care of Mr. Farts, would ya?"

In his room, Glen was sitting at his desk, with a hammer and chisel in his hands. Terry next to him. In front of them was the geode from the backyard.

With shelves lined with a jumble of wind-up robots, plastic monsters, crayons, seashells, machine parts, and walls decorated in movie posters, this was a typical room for a normal boy of his age.

"Hey, Al," Terry said. "Thought your folks didn't allow parties when they were gone?"

"They don't allow friends over when Glen's grounded either." Al smirked.

Terry laughed. "Touché, Al. Touché."

"Anyway, this isn't a party. I just got some friends over. That's all."

"You mean you're having some friends over for a party?" Glen corrected.

"What would either of you know? You've never been to a party in your life!"

"Touché part two," Terry laughed again. "She's got us."

Glen got up from the desk and walked over to his bed. He patted it toward Angus, telling him to come in and jump up. Which Angus was more than happy to do, only he could not jump anymore. So, he just ambled over and slumped on the rug next to the bed.

"So, I guess you want me to keep Angus away from the party you're not having all night?"

"Glen, don't be a baby," Al moaned. "Just do it." Before she closed the door, the jar of moths on the dresser next to her caught her eye. Reaching over, she picked it up and looked through the glass. Inside, the moths were no longer flapping and all lay dead. Dried, curled lumps that sat at the bottom of the jar. "So, you're not just happy ripping off their legs . . . You also suffocated them in an airtight jar?" She looked disappointingly at both boys. "Way to go. You get the humanitarian of the year award."

Glen felt a pang of guilt for his involvement as he looked away. Whereas Terry had not listened, his attention had flitted back to the geode as the desk lamp pointed its bright glow upon the sparkly stone surface.

The Lee sisters laughed raucously from downstairs as a smash of glass rang out, pulling Al away from the conversation.

"Oh shit," she exclaimed, rushing back downstairs, leaving the bedroom door wide open.

With a sigh, Glen walked across the room and closed the door. Angus, meanwhile, had got up from his brief rest by the bed and padded across the carpet to Terry and stuffed his nose under Terry's arm, trying to get any attention.

"Dammit, Angus," Terry complained as he tried to place the chisel on the geode. "Cut it out. I'm working here!"

"He's not hurting you," Glen said, walking back and scratching Angus on his head.

"He stinks!"

"No, he doesn't," Glen retorted.

As if on cue, a long, raspy noise came out of Angus.

Almost immediately, the smell hit Glen and Terry.

"Okay, fine," Glen admitted. "He really stinks. But so will you when you're ninety-eight!"

"Pfft, he's not ninety-eight!"

"He's fourteen. That's ninety-eight in dog years."

Glen then pointed to the other side of the room, and taking the hint, Angus returned to the side of the bed. Lying down with a heavy and pained thud.

Terry turned back to the geode. "Come on, we gotta continue with this."

With a nod, Glen took his stool and watched.

"How d'ya know it's a gee-nobe?" Glen asked.

"Ge*ode*," Terry corrected. "My dad used to have a load of 'em. The outsides are all really ugly and have kinda the same texture. But *inside*, they're filled with different crystals. Loads of different colors. All jaggedy and cool. Probably worth a ton."

"Wow," Glen replied. "How do the crystals get in there?"

"They don't *get in*," Terry explained. "They're made there over millions of years." He moved the chisel over the rock and lightly hit the hammer on its hilt, hoping to crack the geode open with care.

It did not crack.

Another hit. Stronger.

Nothing.

Another. Another. Harder and harder.

But the rock refused to relent.

"Goddammit," Terry moaned. "It's impossible."

"Can I try?"

Handing Glen the hammer and chisel, Terry shook his head. "It's no use. We can try to throw it off the roof tomorrow or something." He paused for a beat. "Wanna go watch the party?"

"She won't let us down there," Glen said, staring at the geode, holding the hammer and chisel.

"We can hide out of the way. Listen to all they say."

Glen shook his head, feeling a sudden rush of sadness. "She hates us. She'll find us and chuck us out."

"Hates us? Why do you think that?"

Glen kept staring at the geode and tightened his grip. "She's changed," he said under his breath. "She just hates me."

With a sudden rush of upset anger, Glen lifted the hammer and smashed it down onto the geode without any use for the chisel. Immediately, the rock split open like a coconut. The two halves then spinning across the desk.

"Whoa there, silver!" Terry said, mimicking the Lone Ranger, taking the hammer from Glen's hand. "How about ya put that thing down before you hurt yourself!"

The geode was exactly as Terry said it would be. The two halves sat on the desk as the lamp light reflected into their concave interiors. Each a mass of brilliantly colored crystals. Breathtaking and beautiful.

But there was something else.

A breeze caught them but not from the window, that was closed, busily keeping the cold out. It came from inside the geode halves themselves.

Terry and Glen didn't really notice. They just stared at the crystals inside, mesmerized with wonder.

Behind them, Angus whined, sensing something was wrong.

Transfixed by the glimmering, there was something at the far end of both halves of this geode. Something their eyes focused on. A darkness.

Something . . . . Behind the crystals, maybe? Then it was gone.

Suddenly, the smell of this impossible breeze caught their noses. A rancid, putrid stench.

"Angus!" Terry exhaled, waving the stink away from his face.

"I think the smell came from the rock," Glen said, still staring at the crystals.

Terry moved his head nearer to the inside of the rock as the smell still lingered. "Maybe," he said. "It's been stuck inside for so long. Maybe it was a dinosaur fart? Trapped in rock for a million years, now released. Just for us."

"Eww!" Glen said.

"Or your dog is gross and did one so bad we smelled it from here, either one." Terry laughed. He then held his half to the light, watched it refracting from the crystals, and smiled in awe.

Glen, though, stared intently at another part of the geode: at the edge around the rock's break. About half an inch thick and a dark gray, he could see something. "You're shittin' me," he said under his breath as he realized *what* it was.

"Correction, that was Angus shittin' himself!"

Glen moved the stone under the light for Terry to see. "That's writing, isn't it?" he said, pointing to the indents that ran around the edge's circumference, where what looked like symbols and letters were carved."

Terry immediately picked up his geode half and

looked at its edge. It had the same symbols and letters, but his were reversed. "That's impossible . . . isn't it?" he mused, trying to figure out what it all meant.

"What does yours say?" Terry asked as he realized he could not read his. "Mine's backward."

"It's weird," Glen replied, squinting at the writing as he tried to read, turning the geode to follow the text. "That's a star symbol. That's a . . . No idea . . . A duck," he leaned in closer. "Then . . . Akka ba es Cthulhu. Go—No that's *Ga*—ene kanpaa . . . manum . . . arduk? Then more symbols." He turned to Terry with a shrug.

"Okay, that's weird," Terry said. "How the hell did anyone get writing in a rock? Even today. How the hell can anyone do that?"

Out in the backyard, under the clear black sky and brilliant moonlight, the filled in hole shifted subtly. The gray grass on this newly laid patch was now totally dead. Blackened. Each blade was crispy and dark as the dirt ever so slightly undulated as something deep beneath it began to stir.

"What do we do with it?" Glen asked, still staring at his cracked geode.

"*Do*? What do you mean do? It's a rock."

"Is it worth anything?" Glen asked, unable to take

his eyes off the glittering crystals within. "There's that place in town that pays people for their jewels and things. Would they buy this?"

"Maybe. No idea." Terry shrugged before changing the subject, obviously now over their find. "C'mon, let's go look at what they are doing downstairs. See what those horrible sisters are doing."

"Al's just gonna shout and send us up here again."

Terry stood from the desk with a confident smile. "It's not *her* house. It's as much yours. Besides, not your fault she is in the room right next to the kitchen! We're just getting some food. Right?"

"I *am* hungry . . ." Glen shrugged as he slowly put the rock on the desk.

After they had left the room, Angus remained. Frozen in place, he stared at the split geode on the desk, wide-eyed and trembling. His ears pinned back as a soft, anxious whine escaped his every exhalation.

Downstairs, the party had somehow become even more subdued. The lights had been dimmed, the music had been turned lower, and everyone talked in calm voices. The weed and booze just made everyone more relaxed and less energetic.

In a corner of the room, besides two tall bookshelves, the Lee sisters flipped through a family album they had found among the other books. Al only noticed when they were halfway through the photos, having only just finished cleaning glass up off the kitchen floor.

The sisters hid none of their disapproval at the pictures.

"My god!" Patty said in horror, staring at a picture of Al when she was six and dressed up as Cinderella for Halloween. "What *is* she wearing?"

Stacy agreed, putting her finger in her mouth and gagging.

Patty continued. "That is *not* her color."

"Give me that!" Al snapped as she took the album from Patty's hand. "I was just a kid, y'know?" With a mixture of embarrassment and annoyance, she placed the album back on the shelf.

In unison, Patty and Stacy shrugged, without even giving each other a cue. A twin act that seemed almost robotic it was so perfectly timed.

Standing from the sofa, the sisters walked by Al and over to where the rest of the gathering were sitting in a semi-circle around the fireplace, which crackled with bright orange flames, Eric's one valuable contribution to the party, as he was the only one who knew how to light a fire. With the windows still open to let the smoke out, the fire was a needed source of heat.

Eric's friend, Brad, was speaking. He held everyone's attention as he was telling a story. A slightly pudgy kid, Brad was very intelligent, though he masked it for his friends as none of the friend group valued anyone's mind. Al was the same as him, having to hide who she was, in order to hang out with the cool kids.

". . . And so," Brad continued as he took turns looking at each person in the semi-circle, taking his time telling his spooky story, "he bent down with his long, razor-sharp knife, and he began. *Slice, slice, slice*, into the goat's neck. Cutting through its jugular as its eyes stared back at him, scared. *Slice, slice, slice*." He spoke the sound effects slowly. Dwelling on the horror as best as he could. "*Slice, slice, slice. He cut the goat's head off as the blood gushed everywhere. Pouring out like a hose. When he had done it and held the poor animal's severed head, it still made a noise. Bleating out of fear and pain . . . The man then threw it straight into the pit. And as he did, *everything* got really quiet . . . Too quiet. And—"

"And he invited everyone over for a barbeque," Eric laughed.

"Aw, shut up, Eric!" Stacy said as she and Patty sat down.

Eric immediately did as he was told.

". . . And then, at first, this little breeze started. Slowly . . . And then it began to grow and grow, get stronger and stronger, faster and faster until it became this huge tornado. The wind spinning around . . . and Tengler? He could hear something under all that noise. Through the wind howling and the cries of the goat still haunting the air came these new voices."

"Voices?" another kid in the group, Andy, asked.

Tiny and looking much younger than his fifteen

years, he had been scared by this story. Visibly scared.

Brad grinned. "Yeah, *horrible* voices, and they were becoming louder and louder. But it wasn't words. They were *screaming* . . . and it was then Tengler knew it had all worked. The old books he had found in the tomb were right. He had summoned the demons from the darkest pit, from hell, to do his bidding . . ."

Just outside of the living room, on the darkened staircase, enraptured by the story being told, Glen and Terry hid.

"Darkest pit?" Eric scoffed. "More like your mom's butt?"

"Shut. The. Hell. Up. Eric," Patty said as Stacy nodded along.

Brad didn't let any of this slow down his storytelling. "Anyway . . . so, all of a sudden, Tengler realized something. He realized that something was really, really wrong. The screaming from the pit. The voices that were getting louder . . . He realized that they were not coming from the pit at all! But they were coming from the house, *his house*. And the voices . . . He only then realized he knew who was making them."

Eric went to speak, to make a stupid unneeded joke. But as he did, he looked over at Patty and Stacy, who both glared back at him. They both mouthed the word *no* to him at the same time. Eric just sank back down in silence.

"So, he ran back into his house, ran as fast as he could," Brad said. "BAM! In through the back door. Up the stairs . . . The screaming was so loud. Not screams of anger but screams of pain. Sounding like a slaughterhouse." All of a sudden, he let out his own high-pitched scream, to jolt his listeners, which it did.

Andy gasped loudly at the jump scare as Patty and Stacy both screamed aloud.

Eric, sitting next to Brad, clutched his ears. "Jesus, dude! Thanks a lot! I'm deaf."

Patty and Stacy then both started giggling. Enjoying this sudden fright. Everyone else just stared at Brad in silence.

"So, Tengler ran up the stairs, across the hall, grabbed the bedroom door handle, flung it open and . . . ." He paused as he looked around for his enraptured audience.

"And?" Andy asked, dreading the answer.

"And then he, Nicholas Tengler, started to scream himself . . . You see, the book was right. It said clearly what he had to do, and he doubted it. One sacrifice wasn't enough. And the screams he heard were his own kids. The hell demons, the ones from the pit, were on his kid's beds, eating their flesh, as they died screaming. They reached out to him, their dad, for help. But he couldn't do a thing except stand and watch. Each of them were too far gone. Their bellies were cut open and all their intestines chewed on. Legs and arms, all the flesh been gnawed off like dogs at a bone. They should have been dead, but the dark magic kept them alive until the demons *wanted* them to die, and the demons loved a meal that screamed."

There are shrill noises of disgust mixed with groans of disbelief among the semi-circle. Andy felt sick, and the Lee sisters were appalled. It was only Eric who found the story hilarious and started laughing.

"That was disgusting," Stacy said.

"It was awesome!" Eric added.

Patty just shook her head. "You made it up. That's no way real!"

"You don't have to believe me." Brad shrugged. "But I swear to God it's true. There really *was* a Nicholas Tengler, and he practiced dark magic."

"Dude," Eric patted him on the back. "Great story, but I'm with Patty. That was BS."

"I'm Stacy!" Patty complained to Eric, mocking being hurt.

He looked aghast, unsure of what to reply.

Brad snickered. "You're identical twin sisters who dress exactly the same. You can't blame the guy, and to make it all the worse, he's stoned."

Eric still looked shocked that he got it wrong.

"Gotcha!" Patty and Stacy laughed in unison.

"Anyway, if ya don't believe me, go to the library and ask for *The Tengler Collection*. Nothing but demonology and witchcraft in there. He was convinced that this town was a big entrance to hell. He had also thought that demons could be raised and controlled. Turning hell to his side. But he had no idea what was really waiting down there."

"The library wouldn't have stuff like that," Andy said. "Would it?"

"Why not?" Brad replied. "Tengler was a famous author who lived here his whole life. They have all his books. He must have left them to the library after he died. And they're all really scary stuff."

"He wrote fiction, though, right?" Al asked, finally brave enough to be part of the conversation.

Brad nodded. "Yeah, that's why he was famous. But they also have his collection of these old books as well as all of his notebooks. And he really did try all that stuff. Conjuring demons, sacrificing goats."

Stacy tutted. "Why would anybody want to conjure a *demon*, anyway? What would he think would happen?"

"'Cause he could?" Brad replied. "He thought they may be like genies in a bottle. That if you freed them, they would be in your debt and would do shit for you. I guess that's what it was. Who knows?"

"Okay, dude," Eric said, turning to him. "Why are you such a dweeb and know all this doohickey about a dead writer?"

"You *are* drunk!" Brad laughed. "We did that book report on a person from this town for social studies. You did yours on the drunk bum who stands in the town square getting his dick out to passing cars?"

A flash of recognition passed across Eric's face.

"Oh yeah! That was an awesome report!" He turned to everyone. "Guy called himself Elvis Presley. Said he was the real king, but aliens stole his singing, so he faked his death and moved to Canada."

Al laughed loudly. She had tried to keep quiet, to let the party just play out, and for everyone to have a good time, she was new to this group after all, but for this, she could not hold in her guffaw.

So much so that the Lee sisters turned to her in surprise at her voluminous laughing.

Eric smiled. "See, someone gets the genius of the story." He turned back to Brad. "My report was true. Yours was definitely bullshit."

Brad smiled. "It's what's in the book. It probably is bullshit. But it's what I read!"

One of the other girls, a softly spoken, demure girl called Lisa, rarely spoke out among the crowd. She was happy just to be included. As one of the Lee sisters' entourage, she knew her place in the pecking order.

"You guys ever do levitation? Talking of the occult, I mean?" she asked.

"That the floating shit they do on TV?" Eric replied. "The magicians all do it. All that illusion stuff."

Brad nodded.

Lisa, though, shook her head. "No, it's a matter of group concentration. It really works. It's called 'light as a feather.' It's simple, but it's really, really weird."

"You bringing school to this party, Lisa?" Eric asked.

"Here, I'll show you."

"I'd like to see that," Al said to Lisa with a smile.

In the kitchen, Glen and Terry have moved from their place on the stairs, and stood by the breakfast table, skimming food from the open bags of chips and pizza slices.

"D'you believe all that stuff about demons?" Glen asked, having been a bit freaked out by that story.

Terry turned with a chuckle. "Believe? In that crap? You serious?"

Terry's dad was a scientist and an archaeologist. His mother had been a biologist. Neither of them went to church, and they didn't believe in any of the religions or any demons, angels, or ghosts. Terry was the same. Just like them. Devout in his disbelief, even though all the heavy metal he listened to were songs about devils and raising literal hell. Though since his mother passed away, he had wanted so badly to believe in anything that meant that she was still somehow around.

"Yeah, me too. *Total* crap." Glen laughed nervously as inside he totally and utterly believed that it could be real.

. . .

Back in the middle of the living room, Brad sat on a wooden chair as six of the others stood around him, Eric, Al, Andy, Lisa, and the Lee sisters. Each bent down with one finger touching the underside of his seat. The rest of the party all stared on in anticipation.

"One, two, three, lift!" Lisa commanded as the group all began to strain, trying to lift the chair up with their single digits.

But the weight was simply too much. They groaned loudly until, finally, they stopped trying, Eric moving his finger away with a grunt.

"Ow, dammit that hurts," he said, shaking the soreness off his finger.

"Maybe he's just too heavy?" Al said.

"Hey!" Brad protested.

Eric laughed. "They got a point."

"It doesn't matter," Lisa said. "We should be able to do this. It's all about concentration and timing. Maybe not everyone's concentrating?"

Brad got up from the chair. "Think ya better find someone else," he said, walking over to his bottle of beer on the sideboard. "I need more drinks."

Al then saw Glen and Terry sneakily walking across from the kitchen. Trying not to be seen as they carried armfuls of stolen snacks.

"Hey, butthead!" Al called out, causing them to stop in their tracks. "You're supposed to be grounded in your room, not down here stealing our food."

They both stared back, unsure of what to do.

"Just go upstairs," she sighed.

"No, wait," Brad said. "Glen, is it? Come here."

At the doorway, Terry, out of the corner of his mouth, whispered, "You better do what he says."

Glen nervously put his three bags of chips on the floor and walked into the room.

"Can I get a beer?" Terry piped up from the hallway.

Al sighed.

"Can't blame the kid for tryin'," Eric said before raising his bottle to Terry. "I like your style, little dude."

Brad motioned Glen to the chair. "Sit here," he said, turning to Lisa. "Be much easier with him, right?"

Glen's nervousness grew. "I don't—"

"Hell yeah, that's a cinch! Dude looks like he weighs two kilos," Eric said.

"Okay," Lisa said as she thought, looking at everyone in the room before coming to a decision. "But it will only be impressive if two do it . . . Maybe just Brad and me? If it's six of us, it won't look as good."

The Lee sisters shrugged and sat, happy to not be doing any more lifting.

Eric smiled, watching as he leaned on the fireplace mantle.

Terry was still standing in the doorway with an armful of snacks.

Brad and Lisa positioned themselves on either

side of Glen. Each placing an index finger under the seat of the chair that he nervously sat in.

"Glen, sit as still as you can, okay?" Lisa said kindly before addressing the room. "Now, everyone, concentrate. Stare at the chair and really will it to lift up!"

The Lee sisters both shook their heads as they looked at everyone else in the room. They thought this was dumb and didn't hide that opinion.

"Maybe we just forget all this and have some more drinks?" Patty suggested to the room as Stacy nodded.

"After this," Brad replied.

"Now, everyone just clear your minds and think about Glen, Okay?" Lisa said. "Think about him as light as a feather . . . Just concentrate . . . He doesn't weigh a thing . . . like dust drifting through the air, catching the ray of sunlight through a window . . . like dandelions in the breeze . . . Weightless."

Despite the twins' annoyance, everyone else concentrated hard. Even Terry in the doorway, still carrying the snacks. Even though he did not believe in the supernatural, he found himself falling under the spell of possibility.

Everyone was enthralled and willing this to work.

Glen, though, was not as caught up in this. He just felt uncomfortable as everyone looked at him.

". . . And on three," Lisa said. "One. Two. Three."

Exerting the slightest pressure on their fingers.

Much to everyone's surprise, even Lisa's, the chair with Glen on, began to rise.

She stared at Brad, who was in awe at what they were doing.

The chair glided up as they lifted. An inch . . . Two . . . Three . . . A foot . . .

Feeling hardly any weight on his finger, Brad smiled in amazement.

"Slowly," she said to him. "Keep lifting."

The party started to gasp and mumble. Even Stacy and Patty were not immune to the impressiveness.

Higher and higher the chair went.

Two feet.

Three feet.

Four feet.

Soon, he was passing the limit of their reach. The high ceilings of the living room getting closer and closer to his head.

"Please, let me down," Glen whimpered, more terrified.

But as he looked down, he saw both Brad and Lisa's fingers had lost contact with the chair.

"What?" Lisa said.

This wasn't supposed to happen. It was a party trick. One her father had taught her. It was all just physics masked as magic. Glen must have weighed about forty-eight pounds. On top of that the weight of the chair, she and Brad only had to exert pressure to lift about thirty-three pounds each . . . Yet it was only now she realized that she had felt no pressure. No pressure at all. Not even from the chair.

"Help!" Glen yelled, drifting closer to the light fixture.

Al raced over. "Glen," she said in alarm, reaching up. But she was too short to reach him. "Brad, help me!" she implored. But Brad was caught staring as was the rest of the room, staring up at the impossibility.

As he hit the ceiling, Glen's body moved out of the chair and pressed against the glass light fixture. "Ow," he cried out as his hip was pressed on it.

Nobody in the room seemed to be able to move.

The pressure of Glen's body increased against the glass fixture. More and more, and the bulb within quickly glowed incredibly bright. Then . . .

POP!

The room screamed in fright.

The light bulb exploded as the light fixture smashed, breaking into shards, showering the room. And along with it, a cache of trapped, burned insects that had been held in its grasp.

As the fixture smashed, whatever had hold of Glen and the chair suddenly let go, and he fell with the shards.

Landing with a thud, the chair broke on impact as Glen fell through it and hard onto the carpet below.

With a scream, Glen scrambled to his feet in a terrified panic. He stood for a moment, not knowing what had happened as he began to feel the stares of everyone here, looking at him with the same confusion. Unable to take any more, he burst into tears and ran out of the room as Al ran quickly after him.

Everyone in the party was silent, in shock and scared, even Eric, though he would never admit it.

The downstairs bathroom door was locked.

Al stood outside, worried. Next to her, Terry was just as confused and shocked as everyone else. So much so he *still* carried the stolen snacks in his arms. Not knowing what to do.

Al had sent the party home, who were all willing to do so after this strange event. Especially Lisa, who could not stop crying as Brad walked out with her.

Al knocked on the door lightly. "Glen? Are you okay?"

No reply.

Al felt so guilty about what had happened. What she had *let* happen. She should have just insisted he go upstairs.

"Glen?" she asked again.

After a slight pause, Glen's quiet reply could be heard. "Yeah," he said through audible tears. "I'm okay."

"You're not cut or anything, are you?"

"No."

His voice sounded so sad.

Not knowing what else to say, she turned to Terry.

Terry leaned over. "I think it's because he cried in front of everybody," he whispered. "He's embarrassed."

Al nodded, understanding. "Glen?" she said. "You know, everybody went home. Uh . . . they all said they wouldn't tell anybody what happened. It scared them, you know. We were all freaked out. Did you hear Lisa leaving? She couldn't stop crying. I think even Eric cried!"

Terry looked at Al in confusion at this last statement.

Al winked at him. She was lying to make Glen feel better, and it worked. The bathroom door then unlocked and slowly opened.

"I want you to call Mom and Dad," he said quietly.

Al smiled as she put one hand on his shoulder. "And say what? Glen flew and broke a light bulb? You think they'll believe that? No, we can wait till they come back, and I'll tell them I broke it by accident. Okay? No one needs to know you broke it."

Glen didn't look sure.

Al continued. "Or do you want Mrs. Vandegrift babysitting you till you're fifty?"

After a moment of sad reflection, Glen mumbled, "No."

"Look, I'll call Terry's dad. Ask if he can sleep over and keep you company. How's that?"

"He'll say yes for sure." Terry nodded.

"Okay, I'll call him and clean up. You can go upstairs and just relax. Everything will be better in the morning. You'll see."

CHAPTER 3

THE FIRST NIGHT

The living room had been cleaned. The kitchen counters were wiped. Food and broken glass thrown away. Vacuum passed around the carpets. It took an hour, but at least the house was back to normal, aside from the lingering smell of tobacco and the lack of main light on the ceiling.

What was she going to tell her parents? That was Al's main thought. She had to take the blame for the breakage. She drew a blank, but it didn't worry her, as she had two more days to think about it.

With the doors and windows shut and locked, she finally made her way up her stairs and closed the bedroom door behind her.

This was a room in transition. It still said *Al's room* on the door, a throwback to earlier years. But now she was Alexandra, not Al. Her room had not fully converted to her newly adopted aesthetic. There was a poster of Madonna, naturally, but also one of a fighter jet. But as she stood here, among the mixed décor, she felt a pang of regret.

In the mirror's reflection, she stared at herself: her teased hair, her abundance of bangles and necklaces, yet she did not feel comfortable. But she was supposed to look like that, wasn't she? That's what all the girls were like.

She began taking off her jewelry, the bows out of her hair, the layers of clothes. Soon, she was standing in front of a mirror without makeup, hair quickly rinsed of the hair spray, dressed in a long T-shirt, ready for bed.

She looked at herself without the paraphernalia of being a girly girl and sighed heavily.

Across the hall in Glen's room, he and Terry lay in twin beds. They both still looked freaked out by the evening's events.

Between their beds, a lamp glowed on a small dresser. The only light in the room.

"Do you want to turn it off?" Terry asked.

Glen looked at the light, unsure. "Do you?"

They both knew each other's answer and, in silent agreement, left it on.

"Hey, watch this," Terry said as he sat in bed and leaned his hands over the top of the lamp. "Look up there."

Glen stared up to the ceiling and immediately

laughed as he saw Terry make a hand shadow of a dog.

"Rrrrrrrrf," Terry said as his shadow dog opened its toothless mouth and barked in time with his voice. "Rrrrf, rrrrrrrrrf, rrrrrrrf."

"Oh, I know one!" Glen said as he leaned over and took over from Terry.

Soon, the ceiling displayed the silently flapping wings of a bird.

It was not long before the shadow of a giant spider from Terry's hand jumped on the bird, attacking it.

They giggled as they engaged in a mock battle between avian and arachnid.

Finally, they gave up with a draw in their shadow war, then lay back down on the bed.

Glen smiled, staring up at the ceiling, where the empty circle of lamplight shone. For a moment, his fear had vanished as he wondered how much of it all was real. In the living room, Brad and Lisa must have thrown him upward, and he hit the ceiling. That was his best guess. He couldn't have just floated. That was a silly thing to think.

In the empty circle, a new shadow slid in from the bottom of the light. It was hard to identify at first from its shape but, soon, became a monster of some kind. Hollow eyes opened in the middle of the shadow as a cavernous mouth opened to show a row of jagged teeth. Then a whirl of tentacles burst out from around it.

Glen stared in awe.

Then, as soon as it appeared, the shape was quickly pulled away.

"How'd you do that one? That was cool," Glen said as he turned to Terry.

But Terry was lying on his bed, his hands tucked behind his head with his eyes closed.

"How did you do that?" Glen asked again.

"Huh?" Terry replied, half in sleep as he opened his eyes. "I did what now?"

The minutes stretched into hours as the night crept beyond its meridian. The darkness, deep and inky, could not grow any thicker within the recesses of this house.

In the upstairs hallway, the void was filled with the rhythmic, labored sound of wheezing, punctuated now and then by the unmistakable noise of breaking wind. Angus, sprawled on his blanket just outside the bedrooms, was lost in a deep, blissful sleep, and his guts continually filled the air with stink.

In Glen's bedroom, the lamp between the two beds was still switched on.

Glen looked as if he were hibernating, in a tight ball, cocooned in a wrap of blankets and sheets, enveloped so completely that only his eyes were visible. He was sleeping soundly and quietly.

In stark contrast, Terry was sprawled across the mattress, half in and half out of the covers that had been strewn haphazardly around him. Restlessness plagued him all night as he tossed and turned, unable to drift off to sleep. The light was too bright, too demanding of attention.

Finally, he had had enough and leaned over and switched off the lamp.

In the darkness, he laid back, finally thinking he could drift off to sleep, when his bladder began to throb.

He let out a soft moan of annoyance as he slouched off the bed, shuffled across the carpet and out of the room. As Terry walked down the dark hallway, across to the adjacent bathroom, Angus did not so much as stir from his rug.

Switching on the bathroom light, Terry yawned deeply as he walked inside, closing the door behind him.

Glen was even deeper asleep, snoring so lightly it was almost like a cat's purr.

In his dreams, he was running through the town with Angus by his side. But this was Angus from when he was much a younger dog, one able to frolic and keep up with him. The sun in his dreamscape was bright and warm as it beamed down upon them. It was a joyous place and time.

Then an unwelcome sound permeated this summer scene, a fluttering, shuffling sound. One punctuated with soft echoing thumps.

Glen slowed down his run as he looked around, trying to locate the source of the new sound, but as he did, Angus picked up speed and bolted. Running down the street, around the corner and out of Glen's sight.

"Angus," he called out after his dog. But the flapping and thumping sound was growing greater. Louder. More furious. Covering any words he could shout.

The noise grew more as strange shadows started to fill the sky above him.

Before he could think of what to do, Glen's eyes snapped open as he was ripped from his dream.

He stared out from his sheet cocoon, into the dark of his bedroom. He took a moment to realize that something had come with him from the dream. Something that followed him. The fluttering and thumping sound. It was here. And was much louder.

Pulling the blankets tighter, Glen did not want to hear this. He was still too groggy to fathom what was happening. He just knew the noise was loud.

The further he got from sleep, the more his mind began to focus on the present. Where he was. What *that* noise was.

He slowly and timidly lifted his head out from the covers and turned to the widow, where the shades had been pulled down. This did not stop the strange shapes on the other side, dancing their shadows across the window, backlit by the moonlight and projected onto the blinds. Fluttering, scraping, thumping against the glass. Glen could see that they were some kind of butterfly or moth, but they looked much bigger, much fatter . . . Wait . . . *Moths*?

His eyes darted to the jar of dead moths on his dresser. Maybe these are the parents outside trying to get in? Maybe then knew what Terry did? Maybe they were coming to get their revenge?

He sank into his bed with nerves as the fluttering noise got faster and louder.

Al was soundly asleep when she started to hear a muffled thudding of music. Rudely awakened, she blinked the sleep away as she tried to focus on the source of the sound. She soon realized the sound was not coming from inside her room but drifting through the floor at her.

"What the hell?" she mumbled as she slowly got out of bed. Looking around, she tried to discern what was happening. As she stepped toward the door, she could hear that it was rock music. Driven and chaotic. In addition to these wild and frenzied guitars, she could hear what sounded like laughter. Nasty laughter. As well as glasses clinking, mixed in with the sounds of people moaning. Moans of . . . *No*.

"What the hell?" she repeated, this time realizing the sounds were in the living room. And there was only one explanation: Glen and Terry had put on the TV, and it was playing something they definitely should not be allowed to watch.

She reached for her bathrobe from the back of the door, but before she even managed to put it on, she noticed something in the center of the room. Something . . . Unearthly. Something streaming up between the gaps in the floorboards: A light.

The bathroom door opened, and still in his sleepy daze, Terry padded out, flicking off the light switch.

There was no music that could be heard here, no party, no angry swarms of moths. It was silent.

In the darkness, Terry slowly took a few steps toward the bedroom, but as he did, he saw something. Something at the end of the hallway in front of the window.

"Glen?" he said groggily, rubbing his eyes to make out the silhouette framed by the moonlight. But without his glasses, everything was a hazy blur.

"Hello?" he said again, still no answer.

The shape slowly moved forward, and as it did, it became slightly clearer. He could see through his blurry sight that it was a woman, in her mid-thirties, her hair pulled back into a high ponytail. She looked sweet and had kind eyes. Her mouth moved as she spoke, but there was no sound coming out of it.

Terry didn't need his glasses. He was riveted to the spot as he stared at the woman standing in front of him. He knew who this was. Who this could not possibly be.

"Mom?" he helplessly whispered.

Her silent mouth turned into a smile.

Terry's stomach sank, and his eyes immediately began to well up. *It couldn't be her. She died. She was gone.* His heart thudded in his chest. His legs felt like they were sinking into the floor, too heavy to move. A thousand emotions surged through him all at once, confusion, disbelief, longing, and even anger.

The image of her smile cut through the bleariness of his half-asleep mind like a knife. It was *that* smile. The same gentle, reassuring curve of lips that had comforted him so many times. But she was silent and surreal in the hallway's dim light. He wasn't sure if he wanted to run toward her or run away from her, terrified that even a single step might make her vanish. His voice cracked as he whispered again, "Mom?"

The figure then crouched and held her arms out to him, beckoning him into her embrace. Her smile was wonderful and devastating at once.

Glen couldn't hide under the covers anymore. The noise outside the window had gotten louder and louder with each passing moment. He quickly sat upright in his bed and stared at the window that showed the forms flitting outside the shade. He then noticed that the window had been left slightly open.

Oh god, what if they get in?

Using all his bravery and all his willpower, Glen immediately forced himself out of bed. He had to not only shut the window, but he needed to see what these things were and if he could shoo them away.

Each slow, cautious, nervous step he took toward that window seemed to be a volume knob turning the cacophony up. The noise of the thudding and fluttering getting louder and more intense the nearer he got.

What am I doing? he thought.

He was not a brave person, and it was unlike him to face potential danger so readily. His breathing became heavier as he got nearer as the creatures outside battered more frantically against the glass.

He just had to reach out and close the window. *That's all.*

Gritting his teeth, despite the mounting fear, Glen lunged forward, reached up under the shade and clawed to get a hold on the window's handle.

Thud.

Thud.

Thud.

They knew he was there as his hand, grabbing for the handle, pushed them into overdrive. Their movements now beyond a frenzy.

As his fingers soon found the metal handle, he pulled the window shut as quickly as he could. And as soon as it closed, the noise from outside suddenly stopped, and the shadows outside disappeared. Like his closing the window cut off all their power.

Rushing back to his bed, Glen climbed in and under the covers. He shuffled over to the far side of the mattress so his back was against the wall and kept his eyes on the window. He was still very scared yet relieved that the creatures had gone, and he was now safe with the window closed.

His breathing soon slowed and calmed, and he felt a wave of relief.

But then a new noise came.

A much worse noise.

Scratching.

Coming from inside the wall behind him.

Al bent down over the light that spilled up through the cracks in her floorboards. The blue beams striped her face as she stared in curiosity. How was this even possible? Below the floorboards should have been a void before it became the ceiling for downstairs. She even used that void to hide her diary, in the corner of the room where one of the floorboards had been loose. But as she looked down, through the floorboard gaps, she could see the living room below.

Hoping that this floorboard would be loose, too, her fingers reached out. Surprisingly, it was, and it lifted with ease. The whole two-foot-long board came up as if it were not even nailed in place. Light streamed up at her, basking her whole face, allowing the whole room to be seen.

It was not Glen and Terry watching loud adult films. It was . . . something else. The rock music play was so loud that its vibrations rattled the room around her. She could see several figures rushing about the room, destroying it. One kicked over a table, smashing it to the floor. One tipped over a bookshelf. But she could not see who they were. They moved so fast they were almost a dark blur.

"Stop it," Al screamed down from her impossible view. "Who are you?"

But they did not listen. They continued to destroy everything they could. Another crash, another bookshelf smashed over.

She then looked across to the far end of the room, where two blurry dark figures were not destroying anything like the others but rutting wildly. Moaning and screaming in ecstasy. But it was not loving or passionate. It was animalistic. Rough. Violent.

The television was then hurled across the room, smashing against the far wall.

"*Stop*!" Al screamed again.

A shriek of delight came from one of the figures as a fire quickly broke out across a pile of fallen books. The flames did not stay there though as they rapidly spread, catching on the carpet then the walls, all within a matter of moments.

"*No!*"

She did not know what to do.

The glee from the figures grew as they laughed and cheered for joy as the ones in the corner moved faster and rougher in their disturbing lasciviousness.

"Please stop," Al cried out again, but her voice

was lost in the raucous cries of joy, anger and passion below her, coupled with the engulfing flames.

Crack!

The floorboards beneath her began to move as if her weight were breaking them. With a distressed yelp, she scrambled backward, making her way over to her bed. Soon, the floorboards where she had knelt snapped away and fell into the burning room. The flames then grew and licked up through the hole.

With a tearful laugh, Terry raced down the hallway to his mother.

"Mom," he cried out, throwing himself into her arms.

He held her as hard as he could, desperate for her to be real.

"Don't leave me," he sobbed as he nuzzled his head into her neck, clutching her tightly. "Please, Mommy. I missed you so much."

His tears flowed, and he blubbed freely. A year's worth of pent-up grief now gushing out of him. He could smell her. That same comforting smell from her perfume. This *had* to be real.

"Mommy, I love you," he managed to say through his stuttered breaths.

He didn't want to ever let go. If he did, she might leave again.

This couldn't be a ghost. He felt her. She felt just

as she was. This was his mom. Maybe there was a mistake. Maybe she had been in a coma, maybe . . .

How did she get in the house? Why hasn't she said anything?

Then something changed.

He then felt her embrace abruptly loosen and fall to the floor.

He soon felt a wave of dizziness as he felt something cold and solid press against his arm. He soon realized he was lying on the floorboards, not kneeling as he thought.

Slowly, he lifted his head from his mother's neck to look at her face.

But it was not her face. It was not her at all.

In his hands, he felt fur.

"No," he muttered.

Where he expected to see his mother's loving stare were the wide, milky eyes of Angus. His mouth lolled open as his tongue hung out.

"No, no . . . no!" he screamed in horror, realizing his embrace to his mother was, in fact, a tight grip around the old dog's neck.

After letting his grip immediately loosen, Angus's body slumped downward out of his arms.

Terry could only stare into the dog's eyes. His dead eyes.

The wail he let out was from the very bottom of his soul. Desperate, primal, and terrified.

. . .

The clawing and scratching behind Glen soon increased as if whatever was in there desperately wanted to get out of the crawlspace and to him.

Cowering, Glen could only stare at the wall, not knowing what he could or should do. It was not like the window. He had nothing to shut here. Nothing to lock.

The clawing then started to move around the wall. Slowly, it scraped and clawed up to the ceiling, then around the corner, to behind the bed's headboard, where Glen was huddled. It followed him.

In an instant, he screamed, then ran for the door.

The flames had spread across the living room through the floorboards. It was an inferno down there. Nothing had escaped the flames. Even the figures, who were somehow still alive, laughed, moaned and screamed amid the blaze that engulfed them.

The fire had now burned away more floorboards, and the flames reached the side of Al's bed.

There was only one choice if she didn't want to perish in this fire: to get out of her bed and run to her bedroom door, across the little unburned floorboards.

Terry could not stop screaming as he stared at Angus in horror and felt a burning in the pit of his stomach.

Time had stopped for him. What may have only been less than a minute felt like a lifetime. The guilt he felt went beyond a mere feeling, and it was almost a presence that consumed every part of him. He could not stop the tears, could not stop anything. He could only scream and weep as he stared at what he had done.

His mind spun at such a rate he could not even form a thought. He could not wonder what happened with his mom. He could not wonder how he mistook Angus for her. He could not wonder anything.

He did not even hear Glen and Al run out of their bedrooms at the exact same time, both also in a screaming panic.

But in the bedrooms, there was nothing. No scratching sounds, no fires. There were only the three of them . . . and Angus's body.

The rest of the night was spent huddled in the basement playroom, the only place in the house that offered a semblance of refuge for them. Gone were the toys they once played with down here. Since then, it was a small living room. A small, outdated television flickered weakly in one corner, casting a banal sitcom out to the room as two old threadbare sofas lay next to each other. A dozen lamps had been hastily brought down here, their light chasing away every shadow in every corner. A comfortable, basic, and very well-lit room.

The upstairs felt tainted to them, haunted by the specter of what each had seen. The living room was also off-limits after the levitation antics of the party. This basement had been unblemished by the night's terror. It felt like the safest room to them.

On one sofa, Terry sat, slumped. His sobs were relentless, aching as each gasp of breath strained out of his lungs. Al held him close, trying to comfort, but he was not alone in his grief. Both her and Glen's cheeks also glistened with tears.

None of them spoke. None of them could find any words. All they could do was cling to one another.

They just had to wait till the sunrise.

And upstairs, in the hallway, Angus's body lay motionless.

The morning soon arrived, serene and cloudy. A far cry from the chaos of the night before.

The front door of the Simon house creaked open as Terry stepped outside, still wearing the same clothes from the previous day. Glen followed him, still dressed in his pajamas. The tears may have stopped, but Terry's was emotionally in tatters. A hollow shell of himself. He couldn't bring himself to leave without confronting what he had done in the light of day.

For the past hour, he had sat on the upstairs hallway floor, cradling Angus's lifeless body in his lap. His hand moved in slow strokes over the still fur, his voice trembling as he whispered endless soft apologies. There were no tears left, only the suffocating guilt. The magnitude of his actions bore down on him mercilessly.

Glen walked behind him, wrestling with his own conflicting emotions. He didn't want to think badly of his friend, but the image of Terry gleefully tearing the legs off moths stuck in his mind. He didn't truly believe that Terry had harmed Angus on purpose, not like the moths, but he couldn't fully shake the simmering anger he felt about it. Even after the three of them had witnessed such impossible, nightmarish things, Terry still did what he did, whether he knew what he was doing. And Glen did not know if he could ever forgive that or what to think.

Before he left, Terry turned around, his eyes bloodshot and sore and his face forlorn.

"I'm really sorry," he apologized for the hundredth time.

"S'okay." Glen shrugged, hiding his own emotion as best as he could. Of course he was devastated at losing his beloved dog, but crying in front of Terry would just make things worse. "As Al said, he *was* really old and could have died before any of that."

Terry nodded weekly.

"You wanna come back over later?" Glen asked.

Terry shrugged as he walked down the driveway.

Did Glen believe Angus had died before Terry held him? Not really. But he hoped it was for Terry's sake.

Chapter 4

The Day After

The previous thirteen months had eradicated any trace of a caring touch from the Chandler household. After his mother had passed away, Terry and his father just continued to exist, day to day. As before, the same tchotchkes sat on the mantle, the same art prints hung on the walls, but neither had cleaned the house properly since the wake was held here.

With his father being an archaeologist, a wealth of ancient artifacts adorned each room. Fossils of varying size, tools, ceramics, pots, arrowheads . . . It was a small museum, albeit one that was in no particular order.

This house was once indeed a beautiful place to live, but it lay as a murky, dusty shell of its former self.

A click sounded as the lock turned, and the front door soon opened.

"Dad?" Terry called out as he stepped inside.

There was no answer.

Shutting the door behind him, Terry kicked off his shoes and walked into the hallway, peering up the stairs.

"Dad?" he called out again. "You there?"

Still nothing. Only a deep silence.

Walking across to the living room, he saw no one was there either. With a sigh, he crossed through to the kitchen. It was no less empty, but it was certainly a lot filthier: a dozen television dinner containers sat piled on the counter as the sink was filled with dirty cups and utensils.

Terry, looking around wearily, noticed a scrawled note on bright yellow paper attached to the refrigerator. With a grimace, he walked over. Reading the note, he grunted through gritted teeth.

Got work. Back tomorrow. Have Fun—Dad.

Glen sat at his kitchen table, staring into his bowl of cereal, moving the spoon through the milk, unable to eat a single bite.

Since Terry had gone home, Glen had wanted to go sit with Angus and say goodbye, but he found that he just couldn't. He couldn't even walk upstairs. He could not face seeing that truth. The loss hit him a lot harder than it did last night.

The sound of the refrigerator opening rattled him out of his thoughts. Turning, he saw Al rooting around the shelves, looking for a snack. She was dressed in the same style she wore the day before, with dozens of bangles rattling with each move and her hair teased up high.

Grabbing an apple, Al took a bite, closed the fridge, and turned to her brother.

"You good?" she asked, knowing neither of them was but hoping he could ignore his upset like she did.

Glen shrugged, staring at his food.

Al walked on over and put a hand on his shoulder. "Glen? It's gonna be okay, you know that, right?"

"Where are you going?" he asked quietly, noticing her clothes, hair, and makeup.

"I'm staying here," she replied. "You sure you're okay?"

"What's happening with Angus?"

Al offered a weak attempt at a comforting smile. "Don't worry about it."

"Please, what are we going to do?"

Al sighed. "Well, I put a sheet over him for now."

"You gonna call Mom and Dad?"

Al knew that question would come. She sometimes forgot Glen was only ten and still very much hanging onto the apron strings.

"We don't need to call them," she replied.

"You *have* to tell them about Angus!"

"I'm not gonna tell 'em on their holiday. It'll ruin it for them. They can't do anything now anyway. All it will do is make them come back. Holiday ruined."

Glen put his spoon down and stood from the table. "Well, if you're not gonna call them, I will."

"Please, Glen, don't be like that. You can't call them."

From the sideboard, he picked up his parents' itinerary sheet and held it up to her. "I *can* call 'em. I got the numbers right here."

"Oh, come on, don't be a brat," Al said, walking over to take back the itinerary.

Glen moved around the table, farther away from her. "I'm calling them, and that's that!"

With a shake of her head, Al walked the other way around the kitchen table and blocked Glen off at the sink. An easy catch.

She grabbed the top part of the itinerary paper, and they both pulled at the same time. Desperate to get the sheet in their own possession.

Within a matter of seconds, the sheet tore in two. Al getting the top half with the phone numbers on. The part Glen needed.

"Give it to me!" he shouted.

But Al was having none of it. She didn't want to call her parents. She didn't want to have to explain Angus. She didn't want to have to explain the light. She just wanted to delay the inevitable.

"Al! We have to call them."

Shaking her head, she scrunched up her half of the itinerary then shoved it down the waste disposal in the sink.

"No!" Glen cried out, staring at it.

Quickly, she flicked the switch and turned on the tap. The sound of the blades turning on and spinning through the paper was sharp and noisy. A few seconds later, she switched it off again.

A sudden knock at the door ripped away both Glen and Al's attention.

She looked at Glen, then to the disposal before walking away to answer the door.

Al knew she shouldn't have let that escalate, but she first had to have a plan of what to tell them.

And she also was expecting visitors.

Glen peered into the waste disposal.

It was dark there. Dark with razor-sharp teeth.

She had only turned it on for a few seconds. *Maybe some of the itinerary is still down there? Might not all be chopped up.*

Cautiously, he reached his hand out and moved it toward the mouth of the disposal. He quickly looked up at the switch. It was fully in the "off" position.

As his fingers brushed past the rubber lip that led downward, he hesitated again. He tried to see in, but it was too dark.

He tried to convince himself he *had* to do this. He had to get the phone numbers out. They may not be destroyed. They still may be in there.

Slowly, he began to move his hand inside the disposal.

A sudden pair of bloodcurdling screams made Glen jolt hack, pulling his arm out of the disposal with a scared gasp.

Turning to the doorway, he was quickly met with the grinning faces of Patty and Stacy Lee, who found their joke hilarious.

Al came up beside them and glanced at Glen apologetically. He didn't need that from her friends.

Turning, the sisters were soon joined by Eric.

"You're so lucky to have your parents go outta town," Stacy said.

Patty joined in, completing the thought. "Our olds never leave. Ever. It's so annoying."

"How long are they away for?" Eric asked.

As Al was about to answer, Stacy said, "All weekend!"

"Aw, radical!" Eric smiled as he nodded to Al. "Thanks for the invite!"

"She can do whatever she wants," Patty added. "Except no magic this time!"

Glen stared at Als friends like intruders. Rude intruders. He couldn't keep quiet. "She *can't* do whatever she wants!"

"Who crawled up your butt?" Stacy asked with a raised eyebrow before turning to Al. "Is he going to be here *all* day?"

"Hey," Glen retorted, "you can't just walk in here whenever you want."

"Guys, come on," Al said, trying to quell the situation.

Terry sat on his bed in his empty house. Like his father's archaeology collection that littered the downstairs shelves, here had a similar collection. Where his father had a tenth-century Egyptian clay pipe found on an excavation to the Gobi desert, Terry had a plastic figurine of a dragon bought from Kmart for two dollars. Where his father had a framed print of a recovered parchment from Pompeii before its eruption in 79 AD, Terry had the poster of "Walk Among Us" by the Misfits tacked above his bed. His father had history, Terry had fantasy and rock music.

Staring out of the window, he could not help but think of the night before. How all the strange events started with the hole in the backyard. That putrid stench that emanated from it. The dead gopher inside. The moths. The geode with that writing in it.

"Come on, Alexandra," Stacy said as she opened a can of diet soda. "We're going to the beach."

"Eric's got his Trans Am outside," Patty added.

Glen sat at the table on his own, back to pushing his soggy cereal around the bowl, avoiding eating it as much as he could.

Everyone else was standing by the counter.

Stacy smiled. "We're gonna stay till dark and have a big bonfire." She slyly turned her eyes to Eric, then back to Al. "Two to a blanket."

Al looked unsure.

Glen looked up from his cereal at his sister. He knew she wanted to go. She seemed to want to do everything with her newfound friends. But he did not want to be alone. Not with Angus still upstairs.

Pulling Al to one side, Stacy whispered in her ear. "Eric really likes you, you know? You gotta come."

"I can't leave Glen," she sighed.

"Oh, just leave him some Gerber's." Stacy laughed loudly. "He'll be fine."

Glen looked up from the table, having heard her comment. "Cut it out! I'm not a baby!"

Before Stacy could respond, he turned his attention to Al. "You can't go out tonight! What about Angus? You just gonna leave him there? And what about what happened last night? You *have to* call Mom and Dad!"

"Glen, please," Al replied, "just cool it."

"What's he talking about?" Patty asked. "The floating thing?"

"No!" Glen replied sharply. "Go on, Al. Tell 'em."

Al looked at her brother, then to Stacy, then the rest of the group, swallowing hard before she spoke. "Angus . . . He died last night."

"What?" Patty gasped. "Your fat, old dog?"

Al nodded.

"And he's still upstairs!" Glen added.

"Ew." Stacy's face contorted to disgust.

"And tell 'em about the other stuff," Glen added, staring, wide-eyed.

Al laughed nervously. "There's no other stuff," she lied.

Glen exhaled loudly. "Yes, there is! Something really scary's happening!"

"What happened?" Eric asked.

"I don't know *what* it was, but there's a guy in the wall! And the moths are at the window. Terry saw his mom . . . . And what about the levitation?"

Eric scoffed. "Uh, that was a magic trick, little dude. Wasn't real."

Glen stared at Eric incredulously. They all knew that what happened last night was not just magic. He had had enough of this. "All of you, get out!"

"Glen, relax," Al pleaded.

"No, you relax," he shot back. "What were you so scared about last night? The fire? The people in the room destroying it?"

Al knew the story of what they each experienced did not sound just fantastical but borderline insane. She could not have her new friends thinking anything bad about her.

"Please, nothing happened," she implored.

"You can't go out with them tonight," Glen persisted. "Please! You can't just leave me!"

"Glen, stop acting like a little baby!" As soon as Al said those words, she regretted them.

Glen paused as she stared at her, hurt and shocked. Without saying anything more, he got up from the kitchen table and ran out, stomping up the stairs to his bedroom.

As the door upstairs slammed shut, an uncomfortable silence filled the kitchen.

Eventually, Stacy shook her head. "Now that was très uncool."

"So, what're we waiting for?" Patty asked happily. "Beach time!"

But Al was having second thoughts. "Look, I—"

"You can't back out now," Stacy said. "You *have* to go."

"Well, I have to do something about Angus. Take him to the animal shelter or something. I can't just leave him up there."

This was all becoming too much for her.

"I can sort that out for you," Eric said with a cocksure smile.

Stacy smiled triumphantly. No one would ruin the plans for the beach. "And us girls will go get food at the mall, do a bit of shopping, and we'll all meet up after he's done!"

Al didn't want to go. If she was brave enough to speak her mind in front of the Lee sisters, she would have stayed with Glen. But she felt too much peer pressure. It was like an unbearable weight bearing down on her. She felt so out of her depth and comfort zone.

Glen stared out the window as he watched Eric carry Angus's body, swaddled in a bedsheet, out to his Trans Am. The sight of his pet being taken away to the shelter made the loss feel more achingly real, and more final.

Outside, Al strolled down the path, flanked by the giggling Lee sisters. They waved as the Trans Am disappeared down the road, then turned away, their laughter fading as they walked in the opposite direction toward the nearby mall.

Turning from the window, Glen walked to his desk, where a family album lay open. Its pages were filled with photos of the Simon family growing up over the years. Group holidays before their parents began taking trips on their own, birthdays, Christmas mornings, all filled with so much laughter.

In every picture with Al, she was dressed in jeans and a T-shirt, even from a very young age, she was not a dresses-and-skirts girl, a stark contrast to her current appearance. Page after page showed her and Glen playing together, always inseparable, often with model rockets as their shared hobby. And in so many of those pictures, nestled among them, was Angus, ever-present, his wagging tail frozen in time.

Glen's finger traced over an image of Angus as he began to cry once again.

. . .

An hour passed as Glen sat there. Eventually, he wiped his face as he stood with determination. He walked over to his closet and opened its double doors. Rooting behind a stack of toys, he brought out a box crudely wrapped in birthday themed paper. On it, a card read:

To Al

For Big Bertha

HAPPY BIRTHDAY

Love Glen xxxx

With an angry expression, he moved back toward the bed and ripped the paper away, casting its torn strips to the floorboards. The box underneath proudly stated: *Compact Rocket Launch System. No False Launches. Take Off Every Time.*

Throwing the box across the room, he yelled, furious. He had saved up all his pocket money to buy this gift for his sister. Now there was no way he would allow her to have it. The box bounced off the headboard and slid down between the wall and the bed. Out of sight.

Glen stared at the gap where it fell for a moment. "Good, it can stay there," he said, upset before storming out of the room.

Walking into the bathroom, he stopped as he stared into the mirror. The amount of crying he had done had made his eyes and cheeks sore. Running his hands under the faucet, he leaned over and rubbed the flowing cold water onto his face. It stung but in a soothing way.

He briefly pondered whether he should call Terry and stay at his, but Glen had always hated the smell of his friend's house. It smelled like dirt, and it was so dusty it made him sneeze. But that was somewhat preferable to being here with all the memories.

"*Glen*," a voice rang out from outside.

Pausing, he turned and looked out of the bathroom window, but after scanning the side return, he could not see where the voice had come from.

"Hello?" he called out of the window. "Who is it?"

"*Glen*," it repeated. "*Glen*."

Shaking his head, he walked out of the bathroom and downstairs to the side door of the house.

Opening it, he peered outside.

"Hello?" he called out again. "Anyone there?"

"*Glen*."

But this time, Glen could hear it clearer. It was not so much a voice but a crystalline sound.

Stepping out onto the concrete, he glanced around warily. "If that's you, Terry, you can knock it off right now!"

He spoke firmly, hoping it was in fact his friend playing a prank rather than . . . something else.

"*Glen*."

This time, it came from above him.

Startled, he looked up. His eyes landed on a long wind chime swaying gently in the breeze above the door. As it clanged, it produced an eerie, melodic tone, a sound that almost seemed to say *Glen*, or close enough to make him believe it.

Realizing it wasn't a person but just a coincidence of sound, he shook his head and let out a quiet, amused chuckle. The wind chime clanged again, and he mockingly echoed its tone. "Glen." He grinned.

With that mystery solved, he closed the side door and walked around to the back of the house, intending to sit on the back porch a while, like he used to do regularly with Angus.

But when he turned the corner and saw the grass, his heart skipped a beat, and his stomach lurched.

"No," he muttered in absolute terror before turning and racing back through the side door. As he did, the wind immediately got stronger as the chime began to clang more regularly.

"*Glen, Glen, Glen*," it moaned as if calling for him more urgently.

Slamming the door behind him, Glen's hands trembled as he immediately turned the lock with a sharp *click*. In a frenzy, he rushed to the porch doors in the kitchen. Throwing the lock there too, he forced himself to avoid looking in the direction of what he had just seen, what had filled him with so much fear and lay in direct view out of the glass in front of him.

And then, as if on cue, the scratching in the walls that Glen had heard the night before sounded again. This time, it wasn't in Glen's bedroom but around him in the kitchen. The sound seemed to encircle him from every direction, every wall. What began as a faint noise suddenly exploded into a chaotic symphony of scraping and clawing as if countless *things* were anxiously tearing through the plaster, frantic to reach through.

Running from the kitchen through to the living room, he heard the scratching had been following him, scuttling along the inside of the plaster as he ran, catching up to where he stood within seconds, encircling him here.

Glen decided right then that he would go to Terry's. He had to run. He had to leave.

Getting to the front door, he flicked the lock and pulled it.

But it wouldn't budge.

He fumbled with the lock again. Locking it, then unlocking a second time. But as he did, the sounds in the wall became louder and scarier.

As he screamed, he pulled on the door. Again and again until, finally . . . it opened.

He fell backward and landed on the floor.

In the doorway, with the door swinging open, Terry stood, looking confused, with his hand raised, about to knock on the door.

Desperate, Glen got to his feet as he quickly realized that the screaming and clawing sounds disappeared the moment the door had opened.

"We're in real big trouble," Glen said to Terry with a rising dread.

. . .

"Jeeeeeeeez," Terry muttered under his breath as he stood in the backyard, staring down. "You gotta be kiddin'."

Glen could only stare with him.

The hole was back.

But the grass around it had blackened and withered as if scorched by fire.

The hole itself had changed, too. Instead of just a small opening where they found the desiccated critter, the hole was now wider and deeper. The walls of it also shone like crystal. Just like the inside of the geode. But there was no rainbow of color here, as all the shiny fragments glittered in a bloodred hue, and the lower parts seemed to move as if the walls themselves were pulsing.

"I don't wanna say the obvious," Terry said quietly as if to not let the hole hear him. "But this isn't frickin' normal."

They both wore a matching look of confusion and fear.

"It came back on its own," Glen stated.

Terry closed his eyes for a moment. "I think I know what this means." He then sighed loudly.

"You do?"

Terry looked down into the hole again and, after a few moments, sadly nodded. "It's demons," he said matter-of-factly.

Glen did not know what he could possibly say to that. This was not the time for one of Terry's imaginings.

"First thing's first," Terry added. "Let's cover it. You got some wood?"

"'Round the side." Glen nodded. "There's the bits of the treehouse."

"Perfect!"

Within minutes, Terry had placed a large panel of old chipboard over the hole. The panel was thankfully large enough to cover the entirety of the gaping chasm.

"What do you think this *really* is?" Glen said, unsure of what they were supposed to have accomplished.

"After that story we heard last night, I still think demons," Terry answered. "But there is only one place that could answer that for us."

"Where?"

"I never thought I'd say this, but..." Terry took a breath. "...we gotta go to the public library."

"C'mon, it was just a story. This can't be a thing," Glen said as he and Terry traipsed up the steps of the small public library. "Why would a small place like this have that kinda stuff? Not like this is a huge city library."

"That's what we are here to find out, Kemosabe." Terry shrugged as he opened the door. "All just guess work until we find out."

Glen had noticed a change in his friend. He was not smiling and had not since he appeared on the doorstep an hour before. And for someone like him, that was strange. He smiled. He *always* smiled. That was Terry. Though he carried around a sadness that seeped across his face.

Across the old wooden foyer of the library, they walked up to the oak reception desk. Behind it, the librarian sat, a woman who appeared older than most of the books. Her demeanor was sour. She was small, with pulled-back white hair and enough wrinkles to make her face look like it was made of leather. Her sharp, narrow eyes were magnified by black, thick-rimmed glasses, which seemed to scrutinize every step every person took as if she were cataloging infractions.

Her thin lips were perpetually pursed, ready to shush the faintest whisper or reprimand a careless rustle of paper. This was not the kind of person anyone dared to cross.

Before Terry or Glen could even speak, she leaned across the desk. "How old are you?" she asked in a quiet yet sharp voice.

"Twenty-one," Terry said confidently.

Not even dignifying his lie with a response, she turned to Glen.

"We're doing a book report, ma'am," he said, unsure. "And wondered if you could help us?"

"Can you show us where we can find *The Tengler Collection*, please?" Terry asked as he tried to sound charming and failed miserably.

The librarian shook her head. "You can't check

those books out. They're part of the library's permanent collection."

Glen attempted a smile to break the tension. "We just need to look at them, ma'am. That's all. Not take them out. It's about famous people who are from here. We were assigned to find out about him by our teacher."

The librarian scowled at the two boys as she was making her decision.

"We promise to be careful with them," Glen said.

"Yeah, what he said," Terry added.

The librarian let out an annoyed sigh. "I shall open the collection room, but I shall be supervising you. Making sure you do not damage anything. Young people and books are not good bedfellows."

Terry shot a confused glance to Glen. Neither of them had any idea what she was talking about.

At the back of the library was the permanent collection section. A cordoned off part of the bookshelves, separated by a barred door, where inside was half a dozen floor-to-ceiling built-in shelves surrounding a large reading table. The room was filled with dozens upon dozens of antiquated and rare books that lined every shelf.

As they approached the gate after a short but tense walk, Glen noticed a small gold plaque on the wall that stated, *The Tengler Collection*.

"Is the whole section all Tengler's books?" Glen asked the librarian in a whisper.

She nodded. Her steeliness abated for a second as

he asked. Obviously, her passion, her *only* passion. "Not like this town would have any rare books, otherwise, would it? Mr. Tengler generously bequeathed his whole library to us. There are many first editions and rare volumes. Though the subject of most of them may not be to my liking, it is a fascinating collection nonetheless."

As the gate opened and they all walked inside, Glen and Terry stared at the surrounding shelves.

"Where do we start?" Glen asked.

Terry had no idea.

The librarian motioned to the nearest bookshelf. "This first shelf," she began, her tone almost reverential, "you'll find books on astrology and numerology." She turned slightly, gesturing to the next. "Here, works on divinatory arts and obscure religions." She moved down the row. "Here, blood magic, curses, and hexes." Another step, another shelf. "Witchcraft, alchemy, and forbidden rituals." Finally, she pointed to the farthest, darkest shelf. "And there, demonology and his own works."

Without another word, she walked over to a far corner of the room and sat at a small table, allowing the boys to look around but not without her watchful eye.

"Gotta be demonology, right?" Glen whispered.

Terry nodded. "I got no idea what most of those words meant," he said, forgetting to temper his volume.

"Shhhhh," the librarian hissed from her corner.

Terry looked sheepish as he continued in a whisper. "I mean, what in the hell is hexology?"

Glen peered at the bookshelves. "I think hell is the right word."

A few minutes later, they were both sitting at the reading table and had totally forgotten that, from the other side of the room, the librarian still kept her judgmental gaze upon them.

In front of Terry was the biggest and oldest book he could find on the demonology shelves. A large eldritch, leather-bound tome with no title, and only a runic symbol embossed in gold on the spine. A runic symbol Terry recognized from the edge of the geode. One that looked like an angular, angry face with horns.

Glen had opted for a more modern book. *Demonic Presences in Middle America* by Nicholas Tengler.

Both of them flipped through the pages of their respective books, looking pale at the sheer amount of text in each of them.

Terry turned a page and saw an ink drawn image of a gargantuan scaley beast, holding a person in his claw, ready to bite their head off with its mouthful of fanged teeth.

"Holy fucking shit," he exclaimed loudly in amused shock.

Immediately, they both realized where they were,

who was watching. They both turned to the librarian slowly.

She was staring back at them, unamused.

Terry could not think of what to say, so he just opted for, "Sorry, maaaa'aaaam."

Gone was the clear blue yet chilly sky across the whole town, as the weather became angrier. In its place, the wind started to whip up as menacing black clouds crept in from the east, bringing with them rumbles of thunder.

Outside the animal shelter, Eric sat in his car, its engine idling softly. He stared out of the windscreen to the shelter's front door, where a large handwritten note was taped onto the glass.

CLOSED DUE TO STAFF SICKNESS.

With a sigh, he glanced into the back seat, where Angus's body was still wrapped up in the bedsheet.

"Sorry, dude," he said. "No room at the inn."

The faint sound of a woman crying caught Eric's attention as he turned his gaze across the parking lot. There, he could see a tiny plywood shack and an old lady walking away from it in floods of tears, wailing hysterically.

Driving slowly across to see what this was, Eric stopped outside the shack as he saw on the door a paint-stenciled sign: *DEAD ANIMAL DROP-OFF*.

Feeling relief, Eric got out of his car and turned back to the rear passenger door. Letting out a low breath, he wondered how he even got here, how he always got himself into situations like this.

Slowly, he opened the door, then lifted the wrapped Angus up in his arms. The dog seemed a lot smaller, and as the sheet fell away from the dog's face and Eric saw his open pale eyes, he could not help but feel sad.

Turning to the shack, he noticed the handle was bloodstained. Freshly so.

"Sorry, little bud," he whispered softly to Angus. "I know you deserve better."

Grimacing, he held Angus's weight in one arm and reached out and flicked the latch, opening the door. He quickly wiped the residue off his fingers and onto Angus's sheet.

Inside, the ramshackle building was dark and dank. Two large steel drums with loose fitting lids sat in the middle. Both of these drums were adorned with large stickers that boldly stated: *ANIMAL REMAINS ONLY*. Stepping farther into the space, he could not help but gag as the rancid smell of decay hit him.

Bracing himself, he had to get this over as soon as possible, or he could lose his lunch and then it would not be just animal remains in here.

Reaching for the lid of a closest drum, he lifted. It opened on its hinge and held its position.

He shouldn't have and wouldn't have done so if he'd thought about it, but Eric could not help but peer inside. It was dark. So dark that only the faint outlines of discarded fur and textile could be seen. Nothing discernible. Just a pile of animals wrapped in blankets and sheets.

Then . . . something in the drum moved.

Didn't it?

Staring down, Eric's first reaction was that someone dropped off a living animal by mistake.

"Hello? You okay?"

Of course he did not expect a response. As he had his arms full, he reached forward with his foot and tapped the bottom of the barrel, hoping it may spur what may be inside to make itself known.

But there was nothing more.

Eric stood still for a moment. Listening intently. There was no sign of life, but there was a sound of dripping coming from somewhere below.

Noticing that the drums were on two slatted wooden pallets and were several inches off the ground, he could hazard a guess as to what was dripping out from these containers and *tap, tap, tapped* onto the concrete floor.

Then came the sound of scraping. This time from within the second drum.

What the hell? he thought as he instinctively reached out to open the second barrel lid, holding Angus in one arm as best he could.

But as his hand touched the metal, a loud sound of movement came from inside it. Echoing and deep. A sound that made Eric step back in shock. Sounds of moving against the inside of the barrel. The scrapes of claws on metal combined with strange moans.

The first drum then joined in the fray, with similar noises coming from within it. And then the barrels started to shudder with the volume of the noise within them.

With a sudden flood of terror, Eric darted from the shack, Angus still in his arms.

Throwing the dog's body back onto the back seat, he hurriedly got back behind the wheel and started the engine. Moments later, his Trans Am peeled out of the parking lot, leaving a trail of smoking rubber along the asphalt.

Eric may not have been book smart, he may not have been any kind of smart, but he knew whatever was in that shack was not good.

Terry had read through many pages of the large leather-bound book. Each page he read was accompanied by handwritten notes to accompany the text that explained everything in clear, understandable terms. The actual printed words were almost indecipherable to him. It was a form of English but one where most of the words were strange or spelled differently.

He gazed over the pages of illustrated ancient symbols, the descriptions of creatures, demons, and devils. Their tongue-twisting names, which he read out quietly to himself each time he came across one. It had pages of woodcut images depicting hideous scenarios of demons, who each looked as strange and unsettling as the last. Twisted combinations of human, animal, and insect. Like the worst of creatures, fused with singular forms. And in each of these illustrations, the demons, in their many forms, stood over the writing or dead bodies of naked humans. Men and women. Young and old. Big and small. All were victims to the monsters of this book.

In one illustration, Terry had not turned the page for at least five minutes. He could only stare at the image. In it, hordes of unspeakable monstrosities slithered out of a hole in the ground and above it was a title: *EVOCATION ANTIQUORUM*. And at the bottom was a set of handwritten words, not in English but something he remembered hearing: *AKKA BAES CTHULHU. GAENE KANPAA MANUM ARDUK.*

He stared at the page, his lips trembling as he felt a chill. Finally, he found the strength to speak.

"You're right," Terry muttered.

Peering up from his book, containing little he could understand, Glen turned. "What am I right about?"

Terry's eyes did not leave the drawing as he replied. "We're in big, *big* trouble." He then slid his book across the table, in front of Glen, then pointed to the drawing. "This kind of says it all, dunnit? You remember those words?"

Glen stared at the words. He *did* remember them. The words from the geode.

"What does your book say?" Terry asked.

Glen shrugged. "It says demons are older than the

Earth . . . But how in the hell would that even be possible? Where would they be if the earth wasn't here? Hell? How does hell exist without Earth? The bible said God created the heavens and the Earth. So, it's not like he created hell, waited a while, *then* created Earth."

"I don't think this'll have anything to do with your god," Terry shrugged.

"What do you mean, MY god?"

"You believe in God, right?"

Glen stared for a moment, not knowing how to answer.

"It's cool if you do," Terry added. "Just I think this will be a bit out of that guy's wheelhouse."

Glen shrugged, going back to what he was saying. "Well, this book says demons are horrible. That Tengler guy wrote chapter after chapter just saying how scary they are. Kept calling them 'Ancient Ones.' And said that if you call one, your only power is that you are the summoner and can forever call them, but you can't control them, and they won't grant wishes."

"Bummer," Terry said with a smirk.

"Apparently, they try to drive you insane. That's their game. They drive you insane and feed on your fear and sanity, messing with your mind. Messing with reality."

"Why would *anyone* want that?" Terry replied as he turned the back a few pages in his big book. "Look at this one. He'd drive ya cuckoo for Cocoa Puffs."

He pointed at an illustration of an extremely grotesque beast. Rotten, with chunks of flesh missing from parts of its exposed skeleton. Its face, a mass of what appeared to be tentacles but were, in fact, its own intestines, snaked down to its open guts. To make it more surreal, its entire torso was littered with hundreds of screaming faces, each embedded in its skin, flesh, and bone. As if they were people imprisoned within it.

"Around where the beast stood lay the remains of hundreds of people. Arm, legs, guts, heads, organs, all in piles around its feet." Above this drawing was a title that Terry attempted to read out. "The Dee-uhl Lord of Ab . . . ab homyn . . . homyn. Urgh. What the hell is with this English?"

As Glen looked at the title, he could tell what it translated to. "The Demon Lord of Abominations," he said. His eyes scanned over the image until he saw something that made him gasp. Something at the monster's feet. "A geode!" He pointed to it.

Turning the page back to the image of the hole in the ground, Terry tapped on it. "So, what is this, then? A doorway to hell? A portal to a demon universe? Either way, I think I was right. It *is* demons."

"My book talks about gates between realities," Glen said. "Said demons use gates to come through to our world. But it doesn't say how or why. It doesn't say much, really."

"So . . . the thing we read from the geode was this right?" Terry said, staring at the text on the page.

Glen nodded. "We did something really stupid, didn't we?"

"Yeah," Terry sighed loudly. "Why is this shit happening to us? We just wanted to dig a damn hole!"

"We need to look at the other books, see if we can find out how to get rid of these things. Mine doesn't have stuff like that in it."

"Mine could, but there's so many pages. And we need a notepad to remember all this stuff."

"Boys," came the librarian's voice as she appeared behind them. They hadn't even noticed her approaching and jumped in shock as she spoke. "It is time to leave now."

"Wait," Terry pleaded.

"We haven't finished," Glen added.

The librarian peered down at them, unimpressed. "You have one min—"

"Excuse me?" someone said from the doorway, an old man, looking lost.

Upon hearing him, the librarian's demeanor shifted to a much more pleasant and amenable one.

"How can I help ?" she asked in a hushed tone as she walked over to him.

It was clear she just didn't like children.

As she was distracted, Glen turned to Terry and whispered, "We need this book."

Terry nodded.

Glen looked at it. But it was clearly too big to sneak out. "What are we gonna do? We don't have anything to hide it in!"

Terry peered over his shoulder to check that they weren't being watched and noticed that the librarian was leading the old man away.

With a wiggle of his eyebrows, Terry quickly smirked as he reached into his pocket and brought out a small penknife.

Chapter 5

Banishment

Outside, the afternoon had gotten significantly grayer. The last remnants of the sun had been fully blotted out by thick, ominous clouds that brought the threat of a storm.

Glen and Terry hurried from the library at a brisk pace. Looking guiltily over their shoulders every few feet, expecting the librarian to come running out after them, screaming like a banshee for what they had done to her book.

When they got a few more blocks away and far from the people who were milling around the town, Terry reached into his jacket and brought out a couple of dozen pages. Pages cut out from the large leather-bound book.

"This makes us bona fide criminals, right?" Terry asked with a grin. "Like we are badasses!"

This was his first real smile of the day. He was distracted enough to not remember the night before.

But Glen did not smile. He looked sheepish and guilty.

"Those Ancient Ones are nothing compared with what the library's gonna do to us."

Terry shook his head. "I put the book back on the shelf. No way she will know it's us. They don't know what we read. Won't be found till the next person picks it up, and by then, we will probably have our own kids." He flicked through the pages in his hand, checking each one. "So, we got that one telling you how to summon the demons. That thing you read from the geode." He turned to the next page. "And right here, someone... I presume that Tengler dude, wrote a translation of those words. Wanna know what it says?"

Glen looked unsure.

Terry read the handwriting aloud anyway. "Ancestor of the Gods, Cthulhu, creature of darkness and pain, I summon thee from thy resting place from the bowels of existence."

"How can saying that aloud in another language do all this?"

"Ah, it's not just the words. That's just the first part. Seems there's this whole ritual you have to go through. You need blood, and it has to be at a certain time of the year. The conjurer has to have not 'engaged in sexual congress' for six months . . . I don't know what that is. You think it's a political thing? They have congresses in governments, right?"

"You cut yourself over the hole, right? You bled."

Terry's eyes widened. Having totally forgotten, what with all the other things that had happened. "Oh, yeah!"

"Urgh, I've got such a bad feeling about this."

"Nah, to complete it all, you gotta offer a sacrifice. Like Tengler did."

"He killed that goat, didn't he?" Glen asked.

"Maybe Angus?" Terry said weakly, his expression immediately falling. He looked through the pages again. "No, he wasn't at the hole. It can't be him. The notes on the pages say that sacrifice is the key to the whole thing. Without it, the demons can't stay and destroy mankind. You can only summon the minion demons and their creator, but you can't summon the real big demons. They don't come until the ritual is done . . ." His eyes lit up as he realized. "Oh, that Demon Lord guy? He's the minion demon's creator."

"So, that picture isn't even of the really bad demons?"

Terry shrugged. "I guess, but it says that he's the lord of blood and the lord of madness."

"I can't believe this," Glen moaned as he kicked the dirt at his feet. "By digging a tiny hole in my backyard, we opened a gate for demons to take over the world. That's so stupid."

Terry was reading the notes on the pages as best as he could. Glen let him carry on for a couple of minutes, not wanting to interrupt his flow as he frantically tried to make sure what happened to Angus was not a key to Armageddon.

He read a passage of handwriting that was above an illustration of a naked woman lying dead on a sacrificial altar. The handwriting was rough, but he was slowly getting used to it. And as he read, his tense face relaxed slightly. "Oh, thank fuck, I was right," He exhaled a loud sigh. "For the sacrifice to work, you gotta offer it to them. You *do* have to kill them over the hole. So, Angus doesn't count. Besides, if he *was* the key, something even bigger would have happened by now."

"So, what's the scratching I heard in the house? Those tiny demons? The minions?"

"Who the fuck knows?" Terry said, holding up the pages. "But it says in here how to get rid of them. So, we can get this sorted."

The shopping mall buzzed with the familiar hum of weekend activity, a mess of footsteps, laughter, distant chatter and muzak being pumped through the speakers around the shops. Families navigated the crowded walkways with exhausted purpose, juggling bags filled with clothes or other unneeded goods. The parents' expressions were all identical. A mix of exhaustion and determination to get out of here in one piece and to corral their unruly children back home.

Meanwhile, teenagers clustered in groups, hanging out in front of trendy stores, killing time before having to go home for dinner. Couples strolled hand in hand, pausing to glance in window displays. The mall was awash with consumerism, screaming children, and exhausted adults.

Across from one of the high-end fashion outlets, Stacy and Patty stood on a bench, striking awkward poses as they stared into the store's window. Their reflections overlapped the mannequins on display, matching their plastic poses as exactly as they could. These sisters were, in effect, trying on the mannequins' clothes in one of the dumbest ways possible, but they saw this as genius.

Next to them, Al stood among the Lee sisters' wealth of shopping bags. Al had bought nothing for herself. She couldn't afford it. Not after the money she had spent on her new wardrobe only a few months before.

"What do you think?" Stacy asked Patty as she struck a post to match the mannequin.

Looking at her sister's reflection, she grimaced. "Dusty rose is *not* your color." She then looked at the pant suit she was reflecting into. "This isn't much better."

"Okay," Stacy exclaimed. "Let's switch."

Al had to bite her tongue. They were identical sisters. Switching would just show them the same answer. But they did not think about that.

After crossing over each other on the bench, the sisters quickly struck a pose on their new mannequin, with Patty looking at the dusty rose skirt and Stacy at the pant suit.

"What about on me?" Patty asked her sister.

Stacy mimed being sick. "That's worse. The top clashes with your skin tone!"

They had the exact skin tone. They looked exactly the same in their reflections.

Al looked away, staring off in the opposite direction. She had not realized it before, but she came to a disappointing conclusion. After spending two hours on her own with the sisters, without any of the other people, Al considered them idiots. And not only idiots but also quite nasty people. Not cool as she had previously thought.

As she looked around, one store behind her caught Al's eye and immediately pulled on her heart strings. Filling her with a deep feeling of sadness. It was a hobby store. The window display was a myriad of model rockets.

At home, in Glen's backyard, both he and Terry stood over the hole. The plank of chipboard still blocked up the deep drop beneath.

With cut-out pages in his hand, Terry glanced worriedly to Glen, then down to the pages.

"Go on," Glen prompted. "What've we got to lose?"

Taking a deep breath, Terry began reading a handwritten section from a page. "Who art thou, Mad

Gods of Chaos? Filth-eaters, vile demons, creators of madness . . . ." He sighed. "This is so dumb. It didn't work the first two times. Why should it now?"

"Just say it, third time's a charm?"

"Okay," Terry sighed. "Who art thou, Mad Gods of Chaos? Filth-eaters, vile demons, creators of madness. You have sent phantoms to haunt me . . . The evil demons. The enormous larvae. The wicked winds. May the gods of abomination depart. May they seize one another. May they feed on one another's flesh. Burn, mad fiend! Boil, mad god! May the spirits of light remember."

Finishing the passage, he lowered the page and looked down at the ground.

They both stared, waiting for something to happen.

"It really sounds like we're just insulting them," Glen said. "Burn, mad god? What does that even mean?"

"I dunno. I guess that's the point. To piss 'em off into leaving? Maybe they hate people talking back to 'em?"

Still, nothing had happened. No sounds. No movement. Only the storm clouds above and the cold wind that drifted by.

"Maybe try it once more?"

"So, fourth time's a charm?" Terry asked before starting over. "Who art thou, Mad Gods of Chaos? Filth-eaters, vile demons, creators of madness. You have—"

"What in the world are you doing?" came a voice from behind them.

Turning, Glen and Terry saw Al nearby. A look of bemusement on her face.

"I thought you were going to the beach," Glen replied, still harboring resentment.

"I was, but . . ." As she spoke, she looked ashamed. "But I ran out of money."

Glen looked very upset at her.

"I bought something, though." A smile crept on her face. "Wanna see what it is?"

Of course, Glen didn't want to see a bag full of makeup, but Al gave him little choice as she walked over and opened the bag out to him.

As he reluctantly looked inside, his annoyance and resentment disappeared as there in the bag was a model rocket kit. He could not stop a big smile cracking over his pout.

"Whoa," Terry said as he, too, saw it.

Al closed the bag. "It's not Big Bertha, I know. But I thought you and I could play with it. Together."

Glen didn't know what to say.

"Are we good?" She nervously asked. "I'm really sorry, baby bro. For everything." Before he could answer, Al's attention quickly flitted back to the wood on the floor and what they were up to. "And what the hell's all this, then?"

"We're banishing demons, obviously," Terry said. "The ones from last night."

"Demons?" Al replied, taken aback. "Really? That's where you're going with all this?"

"I thought that, too, but it's true, Al!" Glen insisted. "We went to the library. It told us how to get rid of them."

She smiled. "You guys are both *weird*. You're aware of that, right?"

"Damn right we are." Terry nodded. "But this is totally on the level. We accidentally summoned some demons like Nicholas Tengler did when the tree came down. When we dug that hole. Found that rock. Read the words. Real demons as well. Just like that story your friend told."

Al looked at the plank of wood. "So, what's under that now? You didn't dig a hole again, did you?"

"Not us. It dug itself." As soon as he said that, Glen immediately realized how stupid this sounded. "I mean—"

"Let's see," Al said. "I wanna see me some demons."

"We can't," Glen replied, unsure of what he was saying but trying to convince himself. "They're gone now, I think. They should be, anyway. We did the incantation a few times."

"Yeah, we banished them with these," Terry added as he held up the cut-out pages of the old book.

"So, you went to the library," Al said, looking at the pages. She could tell they were old. She could guess where they came from. "I don't wanna know where you got those, do I?" she said, pointing to the pages.

"No, ma'am, you do not!" Terry replied with a smile as he rolled up the pages and put them in his back pocket. He looked at Glen. "We should see if it worked, yeah?"

A little apprehensive, Glen crouched on one side of the chip board as Terry moved to the other. They both slid their fingers under the wood, took a deep breath, then lifted it.

Underneath the board, the hole was completely gone. In its place was hard packed earth. There was even some living grass poking up through the dirt.

Breathing a sigh of relief, they dropped the board back down.

Glen then held his palm up to Terry, who high-fived him happily.

"We are demon killers!" Terry exclaimed.

Al laughed. "So, are you both just gonna stand there, or do you want to launch this baby?"

As they walked back into the house, neither noticed the board shudder ever so slightly, as if something was moving deep down in the earth beneath it.

The kitchen was bathed in silence as Terry, Glen, and Al pieced the model rocket together. The horrors they had witnessed, the fear they had felt, and the guilt that had hit them hard drifted into the background.

Each step of the build was carried out with a familiarity, the kind of feeling born from years of similar builds between these siblings.

Glen took charge of packing the recovery parachute into the rocket's body. He folded the material carefully, tucking it into place with ease. Beside him, Al assembled the nose cone, aligning the pieces before securing them together with Krazy Glue. They both could not hide their smiles as they worked. The earlier animosity all but forgotten.

Terry, eager to contribute, had no idea of what he was doing, so he floated between the tasks that Al and Glen offered him. He passed tools, held parts in place and held a watchful eye.

At the rocket's base, Glen fitted the engine, ensuring every connection was tight and secure. The igniter came next, threaded into the engine as Al attached the wires.

When they moved back into the backyard and Glen slipped the newly built rocket over the upright doweling on the launch pad, they were ready. It may have only taken an hour, but it felt like a day to them.

Terry sat on the porch, having stood back from the final stages of the build, and with the book's pages back in his hand, he silently reread them.

"What ya think?" Al said to Glen as they both stared at their rocket.

"It's awesome," he replied as he put his arm around her and gave her a sideways hug.

"Hey, guys, listen to this," Terry said, his eyes

fixed to the pages. "Once set free, any of the Ancient Ones would be all but impossible to control. Many are the unprepared conjurers who have been devoured or destroyed as the demons seek their two human sacrifices to establish their hell on Earth. Mankind has little idea how close total destruction lurks beneath the soil."

Al and Glen didn't reply. They just moved back down to the rocket and did some final checks on the connections.

Terry carried on reading aloud. "The Ancient Ones can only be mastered and the gate closed once again by a true spirit of gentle passions wielding energy derived from pure love and light. Only this pure light can destroy the heart of darkness, which is the substance of the Ancient Ones." He stopped reading for a moment as he looked at what he had read again. "This is utterly batshit," he said to himself with a grin.

"What is that?" Glen asked, having heard him say, "spirits of passions?"

Terry shrugged. "It's all so weird."

Al, standing back, turned to the boys. "Okay, Houston. We ready for liftoff?"

Minutes later, at the end of a stretch of wire that snaked away from the launch pad, Glen was excitedly positioned in front of the battery. He held one of two wires to the terminal and the other in his hand, ready to make the connection and send the rocket sky high.

"Ready, Gold Leader?" he said with glee.

"Ready for liftoff, Houston," Al replied, standing behind him.

Terry looked up from the pages and stared at the rocket excitedly. "This is gonna be so cool," he mumbled.

Glen then began to lower the wire to the empty terminal as he counted down. "Five . . . Four . . . Three . . . Two . . ." The wire touched the terminal. "*We have liftoff!*"

The rocket burst to life with a sharp hiss as its engine ignited in a brilliant plume of flame and smoke.

It shot upward soared gloriously into the stormy sky above, leaving a smoky trail.

Glen stood, his face filled with awe and wonder.

Staring up beside him, Al put an arm over his shoulder. "Nice job, Houston. Nice job."

As the evening arrived, Al was sitting on a sofa in the living room, reading a magazine. With no main light to switch on, the room had a more subdued lighting from the lamps sitting on the bookshelves.

She really wanted to be invested in what she was reading. She wanted to care about the latest trends in makeup and fashion, but as she looked at the words, they held no meaning to her. Every picture she looked at was someone dressed how she dressed, and though she would never admit it aloud, she thought they all looked stupid.

The phone sprang to life with a shrill, metallic ring, jolting Al out of her thoughts. She rushed over to the back of the sofa, racing to the sideboard to grab the receiver.

"Hello?" she said, a little out of breath.

"This is a collect call from . . ."

"Uh, Dad," Michael Simon interjected, his name hastily recorded for the message.

"Dial one to accept the call."

Smiling, Al punched the 1 key.

The line then clicked as the call connected.

"Daddy!" she said happily.

Behind her, drawn by the sound of the phone, Glen and Terry appeared in the doorway, peeking in.

"Your mom's here, too," Michael said, his voice crackling with static.

"Hi!" Marcy chimed in.

Noticing her brother nearby, Al gave him a quick glance before speaking into the phone. "What? Oh! You're both on? Great!"

"How is everything there? Not burning the place down, I hope?" Michael teased.

"No, everything's fine! We're having a great time," Al replied.

"Not too great a time, I hope?" Marcy joked.

"What? No, no, not too good." Al laughed nervously, feeling the weight of what could and couldn't be said.

"Is Glen okay?" Michael asked. "He's still grounded, right?"

Al rolled her eyes at her brother. "Yeah, he's right here. He's been in the house the whole time. He's been . . . lovely."

"How's Angus?" Marcy asked, the question Al had been dreading. "Hope he isn't missing me too much. I trust you're remembering to feed him?"

"Yeah, I fed him," Al said, trying to mask her unease and the sinking feeling in her stomach. "He's fine."

In the hallway, Terry took a step back and closed his eyes, fighting the sting of tears. *It wasn't my fault. It wasn't my fault. It wasn't my fault*, he repeated silently, like a mantra.

"We miss you all," Marcy said warmly.

"Can you put Glen on?" Michael asked.

"Oh, okay. Yeah, I miss you, too," Al replied. She held the receiver out to Glen and whispered, "Just let them enjoy their holiday. They'll find out about Angus soon enough. Be cool, okay?"

Glen nodded sadly as he took the phone. "Hiya," he said, feigning enthusiasm.

"I hope your sister hasn't been making your life hell." Michael laughed.

"What? No, she's been alright," Glen replied.

"What have you been up to?" Marcy asked.

"Nothing, really. Just hanging around. I don't know." Glen's expression then grew serious as he brought the receiver closer to his mouth. "Um, Mom? Dad? There's something I wanted to ask . . ."

Al stiffened, her nerves jangling. *Was he about to*

spill everything? The light. Her leaving him to go shopping. And worst of all—Angus.

"Um, well, could I sleep over at Terry's house? I know I'm grounded but . . ."

Al exhaled quietly in relief.

Terry, now with them again, watched on silently.

"You know this doesn't mean we're okay with what you did in the backyard," Michael said sternly.

"Yeah, I know," Glen mumbled.

His father's tone lightened. "But sure, just be good!"

After the goodbyes and reassurances, Glen hung up the phone.

"Good going, Houston," Al said with a wink.

Burger Shack had been a cornerstone of teenage life in the town for years, a go-to spot for high schoolers looking for an easy place to hang out after school or on weekends. Known for its unapologetically greasy burgers and perpetually overcooked French fries, the food wasn't gourmet by anyone's standards or taste, but it had a charm that kept the crowds coming back. The prices were cheap enough to suit a kid's budget, and the service was quick enough to satisfy impatient teens on their way to the next adventure. Most importantly, Burger Shack boasted a large outdoor seating area, complete with rickety picnic tables and a few umbrellas that offered patchy shade, where teenagers lingered for hours.

And at one of the tables, ignoring the chill and approaching storm, Eric stared down at the two sloppy, sauce-drenched chiliburgers sitting on a tray in front of him. Opposite sat Stan and Guy, each with an identical pair of burgers in front of them, mirroring Eric in every way.

Though they were technically his friends, they acted more like goons, laughing at every half-baked joke he made, nodding along with whatever opinion he voiced and occasionally looking to him for cues on how to react to a situation. If Eric declared these burgers gourmet cuisine, which he did, Stan and Guy would enthusiastically agree, even as the grease dripped onto their napkins, making the thin paper almost translucent as it soaked in.

"Fuckin' weather," Stan grumbled, more to himself as he looked up at the dark clouds.

Guy, meanwhile, was staring at his burgers as he lifted the top bun on each. "Shit," He grimaced. "They gave me tomatoes. I told 'em I didn't want 'em. I hate tomatoes."

"But they're good for ya," Eric joked with a smile. "Make you grow all big and strong."

Shrugging unhappily, Guy picked up a burger and took a bite. His face immediately reflected his dislike of the tomato's texture and taste.

"You know you could have just taken the tomatoes out and ate the rest?" Eric suggested.

With a nod, Guy slowly put the burger down and

took out some chunks of tomato from inside the bun. "This is so disgusting."

"You think *that's* disgusting?" Eric said as he took a bite of his own burger. Not waiting to finish chewing as he continued. "I had to carry a dead dog today."

"Huh," Guy said, looking up.

"Dog? Whose dog?" Stan asked.

"You know that girl, Alexandra? Well, I told her I'd take it to the animal shelter to get rid of it. Which is what I did. But I got there, and the fuckers were closed! They even had a little shack with barrels in to drop your dead animals off. But I couldn't do that. Poor little guy. So, I buried him instead."

"Where?" Stan asked as he watched Guy, still trying to remove all the tomato chunks with his fingers. A messy affair.

"I buried him at her house," Eric declared proudly. "Didn't know what to do. I couldn't carry that body with me all day. So, I went back to her house to put the dog in the garage or something. Leave a note to explain, y'know? And I saw it. There was already a huge hole dug in the backyard hidden under this piece of wood, so I buried him there. Even filled the hole in for them. Bingo. Job done."

They chuckled, tucking into their burgers as Guy got more and more covered in chili sauce, rooting around for the remaining tomatoes.

CHAPTER 6

THE SECOND NIGHT

A Monopoly board lay on the coffee table as Glen, Terry, and Al sat around mid-game. The living room was warm and cozy, with the lamp lights casting their comforting glow around.

Having rolled the dice, Al moved her piece around the board, speaking the numbers aloud.

". . . Six . . . seven . . . eight." She sank down as she saw where she landed. "Oh shit," she grumbled. "You're too good at this, Terry."

"He's just lucky," Glen said.

She had landed on one of Terry's properties. One with two houses on.

Terry beamed as he picked up the title deed card and read aloud. "Alright. Rent is two hundred-forty, and with two houses . . . that makes it eight hundred." He could not hide his glee. "But I'll tell you what, I'll take the Reading Railroad, and we'll call it even."

"Oh, you're such a turd monster," she replied, laughing.

A sharp rapping at the back door shattered the jovial atmosphere, slicing through their conversation. Three distinct raps that echoed through the kitchen and into the living room.

"Who the hell is that?" Terry asked.

Glen looked at his sister, confused. "Was that the *back* door?"

"Only one way to find out," Al mumbled as she stood to walk through to the kitchen.

"Look at who it is through the window first," Glen called out as she disappeared from view.

"Yes, *Dad*."

Glen turned to Terry with a look of worry. "You don't think it could be . . . y'know?"

"A demon?" Terry asked. "I don't think those things would knock on doors to come in."

A sudden slam could be heard as the back door flung open against a countertop, quickly followed by overexcited screams and giggles. It meant only one thing.

"It's worse than demons," Glen said, deflated. "The Lee sisters."

Terry moaned in annoyance.

Appearing in the doorway, both sisters carried overnight bags as they spoke excitedly.

". . . And we got there just before they closed, and we got the last can of blue Frost & Tip," Stacy said at a million miles a minute.

Patty was just as bad. "And guess who I saw there. I swear it was Scott Baio. Right there, in *our* mall."

Al laughed politely. "I'm sure it wasn't him."

Glen paled as he stood and watched them walk in, unable to disguise his annoyance. "I thought you were going to the beach tonight?"

Stacy turned with a sneer. "We thought we should come over to help with your toilet training."

Al looked at Glen, ignoring Stacy's jibe. "It was too cold at the beach. Looks like it's about to rain."

"So, instead, we're having a slumber party," Patty announced as she pointed to Glen and Terry playfully. "And you're not invited."

Glen looked annoyed at the people who intruded on what he considered was a great night.

Something that Al felt, too. But she just stood there, stuck. She couldn't say no.

With that, Stacy grabbed Al by the arm. "Let's go up to your bedroom," she said happily as she led Al to the stairs, with Patty following.

When they were out of sight, Glen grunted in anger as he kicked the coffee table, sending the Monopoly pieces across the board.

"What you wanna do?" Terry asked.

Glen stared at the game and sighed. Bending down, he began to pack it all back up into its box. The night ruined before it began.

. . .

"When are you staying at mine, then? Tomorrow?" Terry asked, holding a flashlight into the large storage closet on the first floor. "Your parents okayed it, right?"

Glen stood on a small ladder as he slid the Monopoly game among the piles of other board games.

"Yeah, they did. I asked in case someone saw us out earlier. I could say I was on the way to yours."

Terry looked confused. "So, you're *not* coming over?"

Glen looked down from the ladder. "It was the cover story, but I can still come over tomorrow if you want. I was gonna come over to yours earlier before you showed up at the door." He turned back as he finished putting the box away.

Terry nodded with a shrug as he moved his light across the cupboard. To his left was a long leather case propped against the wall, its zip half open. Curiously, he shifted the light, then opened the zip more to get a better look at what was inside. "Wow," he said as he reached his hand in the long case and pulled out a rifle. "Now this is *awesome!*"

"Don't touch that," Glen said in shock, looking down. "That's my dad's! We're not supposed to touch it ever!"

"I'm just looking," Terry retorted. "I'm not loading it."

"Please put it back."

Hurried sliding the rifle back in the case, Terry

relented. "Okay, okay. Don't have a cow, dude." Zipping the case back up, he motioned to it. "That better?"

Glen nodded.

Terry then changed the subject as he aimed the flashlight to the shelves. "Anything else up there we can play?"

"I dunno." He turned to look at the top shelf. Rummaging his hand across, moving a box aside, Glen accidentally pushed it too far, which caused it to tumble off, taking other boxes down with it. Each fell around Terry.

"Way to go, doofus," Terry said, looking at the boxes at his feet. One of them, a gift-wrapped box, the biggest box, stood out. "Hey, this is for you," he said, picking up the box and turning the label up to Glen.

Houston! We have a present!

Have an awesome birthday as you go Bang Zoom to the Moon!

—Al

"But it's not my birthday for six months. It's hers before mine." Glen stepped off the ladder. "Why would she buy me anything now?"

"Good thing it didn't land on my head when it fell," Terry chuckled. "It's heavy as all hell."

Glen stared at the label and then the box, feeling its weight.

"Let's open it," Terry said with a playful malevolence. "Just a peek. No one will know."

Presents were Glen's weakness. No matter how hard he tried to resist them, he couldn't stop himself from opening the ones that had his name on. Every Christmas followed the same pattern. By the time the big day arrived, he already knew exactly what each box under the tree held. When he was younger, it was painfully obvious he'd peeked inside them, earning him plenty of lectures. But as he grew older, Glen became a master at carefully unwrapping and resealing gifts so perfectly that no one suspected a thing.

"Why would she hide it here?" Terry asked. "Not like she hasn't got a bedroom."

At that moment, Glen knew exactly what this was. It had to be something to do with rockets. Since the fiasco a few years ago, when one accidentally launched in his room, his father declared all bedrooms were rocket-free. If she was hiding a present here, it *had* to be rocket related.

Quickly, Glen walked to his bedroom, holding the large box as Terry kept a watch close behind. Rushing to his desk as Terry closed the door, Glen brought out a small penknife from his drawer.

Slowly, he sliced through the sticky tape, careful not to tear any paper or bunch the tape up. When cut, though, he moved to the other two bits of tape and repeated the process. Then, he slowly unfolded the paper, ensuring no other folds or creases were created.

Terry watched impressed. "You're like a spy!"

"My name's Simon," Glen replied in a terrible Sean Connery impersonation. "Glen Simon."

The box was plain brown, with no clues as to what it held inside.

As Glen lifted the lid, Terry came over, eager to see what was inside.

Moving the balls of scrunched up paper packing aside, Glen's jaw dropped.

"Wow," Terry said.

"It's Big Bertha," Glen almost screamed in joy as he stared at the huge rocket. Much bigger than the one they had fired earlier. Almost a yard long and with its thick circumference, it looked professional and very dangerous. "She *didn't* throw it out." He stared at the rocket lovingly. "She saved it for me."

"Shall we set it off?"

Glen shook his head. "Even if I wanted to, I couldn't. I've got no idea how to launch it."

"Hey," Al called from outside of the bedroom door. "You guys in bed yet?"

"Almost," Glen replied in a sudden panic, hurriedly putting the rocket back in the box. "We gotta put it back."

Hearing a commotion, Al opened the door, the Lee sisters behind her. She wore a plastic smock, and her hair was covered in a foam.

"What are you doing?"

Glen, caught in the middle of a flurry of emotions, was frozen. He had no idea what to do.

She then saw the box with Big Bertha and the cut-off wrapping. "Oh, Glen," she sighed.

"Alexandra?" Stacy asked. "Your rinse . . . We need to wash it out."

"You *ruined* the surprise," Al continued, her feelings hurt. "Why did you go snooping like that?" She marched over, picked up the box, and looked at Glen, disappointed. "You should both go to bed."

"But, Al," Glen started. But he had no real excuse. He had been caught red-handed.

"Nice going, Ace," Patty said with a cruel cackle.

"Beddie night nighttime, Glenny Wennie!" Stacy added.

Terry could only stare in surprise at everything as Glen nodded quietly in shame.

Soon, the bedroom door was firmly shut as Al and her friends left, taking Big Bertha with them.

"Let's just call it a night," Glen said despondently.

Terry wasn't tired physically, but he was emotionally exhausted. He had hidden a lot from everyone today and even himself. Being back in this house after the previous night's horror was not what he wanted. But he was too scared in his own empty house to stay there. At least here, he had Glen. He had tried to laugh through it, but even as he got into the bed, he could still see Angus's old hairs on the sheets, not to mention the smell of him permeating the house.

Soon, in his pajamas, Terry lay there in torment. *What am I doing?* he thought. *My house may be empty, but it was away from this. I should have stayed there. It's too soon to be here.* But it was too late to do anything about it. So, he tried to distract himself by focusing on what happened with Al. "Those Lee sisters are awful," he said, staring blankly at the ceiling.

Glen nodded as he got into his bed. "She's probably gonna throw it away for real now. Don't blame her." He closed his eyes for a second. "Why did I open it?"

"She was a lot nicer before," Terry added, remembering the Al that once got into lots of hijinks with them, despite her being older.

The lamp stayed on. Neither of them discussed it, but both did not want to be in the dark.

Later, after the Lee sisters had worn themselves out, they lay asleep on a makeshift double bed on the floor of Al's bedroom. Each wore headphones plugged into the same Walkman so they could listen to the same music as they slept. Identical twins in look, clothes, and in this as well.

Faint, tinny music from them drifted across this otherwise silent room as Al lay in her bed staring into nothing. Her room was a bit of a mess, with remnants of junk food strewn around, clothes in piles from where they had gone through Al's cupboard and makeup items left all over the desk.

Al closed her eyes, wishing the events of the past

couple of days would simply vanish, and she longed for a dreamless sleep.

Shadows are a curious thing. They are nothing within themselves but are instead a whisper of another presence, a person's dark frame stretching across concrete before they even come into view or the earth's shadow slipping over the moon to shape a crescent. Neither fully tangible nor entirely absent, shadows exist in a liminal space where they exist and don't. Where they conceal yet reveal. They can hide things within their darkness, yet they betray the presence of what casts them.

But in the Simon house, a shadow moved around. As Al, Glen, Terry, and the Lee sisters slept, a darkness crept across the ground floor. Over the cut-out pages of the antiquarian book resting on the living room coffee table. Over framed pictures of the family leading up the staircase. Across Al's bedroom door, down past the bathroom, and up to Glen's bedroom.

There, the shadow sat for a moment, listening. Sensing.

On the other side, Glen was fast asleep. He did not see the shadow creep in through the gap under the door. Nor did he notice it drift across his bed and over his face as it moved over to the window. When its darkness hit the roller shades, the fabric reacted immediately with a snap, and it shot up and spun around the roller, flapping noisily through the silence.

Glen jumped out of his sleep with a start. Instantly wide-awake, he sat in his bed, disoriented as he looked around the room. The bedside lamp that had been left on was somehow off. Leaning across, Glen flicked the switch. Nothing. He tried again. Still nothing.

The familiar, eerie, fluttering sound from the night before then started again. Quieter but there. The flapping of wings, the thudding of soft bodies against glass.

Scared in the darkness, Glen glanced over to Terry who was sleeping deeply. He was turned away, toward the wall.

"Terry, you awake?" Glen whispered.

No reply.

Before he could call out louder to his friend, the sound of thudding grew instantly stronger, dragging his attention back to the window. Where he imagined large dark things bashing against the glass, casting their monstrous shadows inwards onto the floorboards below. But he could see nothing. He could only hear it.

Against all better judgment, Glen moved his legs off the bed and stood. The cold wooden boards beneath his bare feet felt almost painful as he slowly walked around the bed, past Terry's and over to the window.

As he got closer, Glen could still not see the moths he thought were there. Peering outside, he looked up, left and right. There was nothing. Staring down, he saw the yellow-bulbed porch light a foot below this window, having been accidentally left on. Its orange incandescence glowed in the darkness outside as a couple of small moths played around its bulb. They spun and twirled in a frenzy until, occasionally, one moth broke its formation and flew higher before lightly thumping against the bedroom window then flying back down to the bulb.

With a wave of relief, Glen shook his head, chuckling quietly to himself. How absurd it was to think those oversized shadows belonged to giant monster moths? He must have dreamed it. His imagination had truly run wild. Smiling at his foolishness, he let out a soft sigh and reached for the shade cord. Pulling it down to cover the window, he lightly released his grip, only for the automatic catch to fail.

The shade snapped back up, rolling loudly.

Muttering, Glen grabbed the cord again. He pulled it down, this time, giving the shade a few firm wiggles as it reached the bottom, hoping the catch would finally kick in, and for a moment, it did seem to hold, but then it slipped free and shot back up again.

And there it was.

Not just a moth but a monstrosity.

It hovered outside the window, grotesque and impossible, nearly twice Glen's size. Its tattered wings, mottled with sickly shades of gray and black, beat loudly. Its bulging, multifaceted eyes reflected the pale yellow of the porch light below.

This creature was drenched in blood. Dripping down its heaving thorax, thick, viscous strands down its spindly legs.

The sound of its enormous wings, furious and unrelenting, filled the air with a droning hum. It was not just a creature; it was a nightmare. And with each beat of its wings, the dripping blood spattered across the glass and trailed downward in thin streaks.

Glen stood, too scared to scream, wide-eyed as he tried to understand what he was seeing. He wanted to cry for Terry, but if he didn't wake up with the deafening noises they made, he sure as hell wouldn't wake up for a panicked cry.

Looking closer, Glen could see that this moth was not alone. Crawling all over its body were thousands of other tiny insects. Moving black dots that rushed all over it.

But the focus of Glen's stare was this creature's proboscis. The long fleshy feeding tube below its eyes as it twitched erratically, pressing and scraping against the glass, leaving red streaks in its wake.

Then something changed as the proboscis began to fold in on itself until what could be seen below, appeared to be a mouth. A human mouth. A mouth whose lips quivered hideously at him.

Lunging forward, Glen grabbed the shade cord once more and yanked down it hard.

Instead of the shade rolling down, the whole window then buckled inward. The glass shattered into hundreds of tiny razor-sharp shards as the moth slammed into it with incredible force. As the human-sized moth pushed its way inward, its wings were deafening beat at speed.

The shattered fragments of glass that burst out did not fall and hit the floor. Instead, as they broke off the window pane and each transformed into something else, they changed into normal-sized moths, all of which flew toward Glen.

Finally finding his legs and his voice, Glen let out a terrified cry, and he turned and raced out of the room. Leaving Terry asleep in bed. Too afraid to stop and grab him.

Yanking the door open, with the giant moth and his squadron in pursuit, Glen charged down the hall toward his sister's room, then slammed his door behind him.

"Al," he screamed. "Al, help!"

Just as he got to her bedroom as the drone of the moths sounded closer and closer, her door opened.

The drone stopped.

Al stood in the doorway, half awake and bleary-eyed. "What are you screaming about?" she asked, looking at the distress on her brother's face.

"The moths! They're back," he screamed, looking behind him, expecting them to burst from his room and into the hallway at any point.

"Huh? Moths?" She looked out into the hallway. Nothing. The house was quiet.

Glen turned back down the hallway again, and as he did, he realized the sound was gone. "They came back. They broke in the window," he whimpered in confusion as he burst into tears. "I left Terry there."

Glancing over her shoulder, Al saw the Lee sisters were still in their Walkman oblivion. The noise of Glen screaming did not make it past their headphones.

Walking into the hallway, she closed her bedroom door behind her. Putting one arm around the sobbing Glen, she spoke softly. "Sounds like it could have been just a nightmare, yeah? How about we go have a look?"

"No," he cried, pulling back on her arm. "They're in there. I saw them!"

"Listen," Al persisted. "Really *listen*. Can you hear anything?"

Glen listened, but even though he could not hear them anymore, it did not stop him from believing they were back.

"Come on," Al said. "I'll go in first. You'll see."

One slow step at a time, Al led them down the hallway. She was *sure* this must have been a nightmare, just as she was sure that last night's strangeness must have been something as equally rational. They all saw separate things that were not really there. Things that disappeared as soon as they ran away from them. Things that did not leave a trace in daylight. They must have all been nightmares or group hallucinations? A gas leak? But now, walking toward Glen's room, seeing the abject fear in his eyes, she was not so sure it was nothing. Yet there was no sound except for their own shallow breaths and cautious footsteps.

Getting to the door, Al swallowed hard before reaching out and gingerly placing her hand on the handle.

The handle was stuck.

"Terry?" she called out as she knocked. "Terry? Are you okay?" She turned to Glen with a concerned look. "This better not be a joke, little bud."

Glen shook his head, the fear still consuming his expression.

Click.

The door unlocked. But Glen's eyes widened.

"Al?" he said, terrified.

"What is it?"

"My door doesn't have a lock on it."

Instantly, a cold feeling of horror spread over them. *He is right*, she thought. *None of the doors have locks.*

She pushed down on the handle with trepidation, then pushed open the bedroom door.

"Terry?" she called out, not wanting to step in.

The room was dark and deathly silent.

There were no moths, but she could see from the doorway that the window had indeed been shattered inward. The floorboards were littered with broken glass, and the roller shade was strewn unraveled in a heap.

They could also see from the dull light coming in

from outside that Terry was still asleep in his bed, exactly as Glen left him, breathing loudly.

"Terry?" Al said in a hushed tone so as not to alert whatever else could be in here.

Slowly, they approached the bed, but Terry did not stir.

"Terry?" Glen tried, speaking louder, keeping an eye on the shattered window.

Al looked around the room again before she reached out and gently shook Terry's shoulder. "Hey, doofus, wake up." Pulling on his shoulder, Al turned Terry over to face them.

He looked perfectly normal. Peaceful. Asleep.

Al shook him harder. "Terry? Wake up! Wake up! Wake up!"

A sudden noise from the hallway startled them. It was the toilet flushing.

A few moments of confusion later . . .

"What's going on, guys?" Terry said, walking into the room behind them, disheveled and groggy.

Al and Glen froze in a terrible fear as they stared at the approaching Terry.

"Guys? What's going on?"

Slowly, Al turned back to the bed. Back to what she had seen as a sleeping boy.

Glen could not turn. He just closed his eyes, dreading what was about to happen.

What had just been a sleeping Terry was no longer anything remotely innocent.

Al's trembling hand was resting on the shoulder,

not of a boy but of a creature. A snarling abomination, grotesque in every detail. Its flesh a patchwork of raw, oozing wounds and its misshapen features, twisted and gnarled. Browning jagged teeth gnashed within a mouth almost too wide for its head as its sunken eyes glowed a deep green.

The real Terry could see this, too, as his face drained of color. He recognized the face of this beast. The same hideous thing that was illustrated in intricate, terrifying detail on one of the stolen pages of the old book. This was no coincidence. This was it, that same creature. That same demon.

Al's hand jerked away, and she let out a scream. Glen could not avert his gaze any longer as he turned and opened his eyes. As he saw the demon snarling on the bed, he screamed, too.

Before they could run, the bed suddenly quaked with violent, sickening speed. From beneath it emerged a dozen scaly, clawed hands. Each the size of a child's arm, with gnarled fingers tipped with razor talons. These hands surged toward Al and Glen, desperately grabbing the air.

Al dragged Glen backward, stumbling toward the door. Their screams mingled with the guttural growls and hideous demonic voices that emanated not just under the bed but from within the walls of the house.

The three didn't pause to see what would happen next. Terror drove them away, and they bolted out the room, slamming the door behind them.

They were not there to witness as the demon on

the bed chuckled as its body began to break apart of its own accord. Blood and gristle snapping as whole chunks of its body separated, and from them grew clawed hands. Soon, the body had split into many pieces, all of which stood as small, separate, hairless demons.

In the hallway, the door to Al's bedroom opened as the Lee sisters, both barely awake, walked out, having heard the screams over their music.

"What's going on?" they asked in worried unison as Al, Glen, and Terry approached in a panic.

"Run!" Al shouted.

At that moment, the monstrous voices and growls became louder and louder and filled the walls around them.

Both unsure of what was happening, the sisters screamed and followed the others downstairs in a hysterical frenzy. As they all ran, the voices in the walls followed them, growing louder and louder, angrier and angrier, scarier and scarier.

They dashed off the bottom step toward the front door.

Glen was there first as he reached out and grabbed the doorknob. He flung the door open wide, and all five spilled out onto the porch, into the night air.

Coming to a shocked halt before they got to the grass, they stared at what was now in the driveway.

Standing next to their car, in the glow of the porch light, was Michael and Marcy Simon.

"Mom! Dad!" Glen cried out.

His parents smiled warmly as he raced down the drive toward them. Throwing his arms around his father, he had not been so happy to see anyone in his whole life.

But Michael did not return the smile. As his son held him, Michael's face distorted into a cruel, horrific expression.

"You have been a bad, bad boy," he said in a monstrous growl. And as he spoke those words, thick dark blood started to pour out from his mouth, nose, ears and eyes. "So bad you need to be punished," he said.

It said.

"*Punisssshheed*," Marcy then bellowed at Glen.

She, too, had turned as monstrous and inhuman as Michael, with blood streaming out from every part of her head.

These two mockeries of his parents both started to laugh diabolically as Glen wrenched himself away out of the demon's arms and raced back to the porch.

"*Punished, punished, punished*," the nightmare version of his parents began to scream like a mantra. And with each iteration of the word, they took a stilted step forward. Their hands now clawed were outstretched, beckoningly. "*Punished, punished, punished*."

Scrambling back into the house, Al slammed the door shut. And as she did, the shutters on every window also slammed shut in unison, locking them in as they created a deafening bang.

The voices and roars in the walls had also not abated and were louder and more vicious than ever.

Glen, Terry, and Al stared at each other in dismay as the Lee sisters carried on screaming, having not stopped since they left the bedroom.

There was no time to think as every lightbulb began to flicker on and off in a rapid pulse. On, off, on, off, until every one of them exploded in unison. A smashing pop that reverberated through every room, throwing glass and filament everywhere as it plunged the whole house into darkness.

CHAPTER 7

MINIONS & HAILSTONES

"What're we gonna do?" Al screamed, trying to be heard over the moans and scratching that surrounded them in the darkened hallway. The noises seeped from every surface, a choir of evil screaming, desperate to break out. Their cries were almost matched in volume by Stacy and Patty Lee, who were still screaming.

Al raced over to a side dresser by the door, pulled open a drawer, and took out a pair of flashlights. Flicking one on, she passed the other to Glen. She then turned the beam onto the screaming Lee sisters, casting them into a bright spotlight as they held onto each other. "Would you two shut the *fuck* up!" Al shouted as loud as she could. "We need to focus!"

Immediately, the sisters fell silent, shocked by Al's demand.

"We could try going out the back!" Terry

suggested, finding it hard to speak over the noises from the walls.

With a nod, they all began to walk toward the kitchen, keeping as close together as they could.

Reaching the back door, they couldn't see anything bad through the glass. The yard looked as it should do.

"I don't see anything," Glen whispered, shining his light onto the grass.

As he spoke, all the noises, the moaning and the scratching from every wall, started to fade out. Causing them to freeze on the spot. The Lee sisters whimpered loudly, clutching to one another in terror.

"H-Have they g-gone?" Stacy asked.

"Get the door," Glen suggested, ignoring the question.

With a nod, Al grabbed the handle, but just like the bedroom before, it would not budge.

"Shit," she seethed. She tried to unlock the mechanism. "It's stuck."

"Come on," Terry said, impatiently scared.

"Hey, I tried!" She replied as she gave up. "You give it a go."

Glen and Terry each then tried in turn, but both failed to budge the lock or open the door.

"I'll try the side door," Al said as she moved over to the other side of the kitchen. But that door was also stuck.

"It wants to keep us in here," Terry sighed under his breath.

The Lee sisters started to blub even more. Tears streamed down their cheeks. Their cries were grating on everyone else in the room.

"Goddammit," Al grumbled. "There's no time for that."

Finally, with Terry trying as hard as he could to open the back door, the handle clicked loudly under his weight, turning down, causing the door to unlatch and swing open.

None of them waited to run outside.

As their feet hit the concrete, and they saw that no demons were waiting out here, a small wave of relief fell over the group.

But then Patty started to scream again. Closely followed by Stacy.

"Oh, come on, guys!" Al complained as she turned her gaze to where they were staring.

There, past the porch, at the end of the backyard, was a thick group of shadows in front of a hedgerow.

"What's that?" she whispered as she aimed her torch toward it.

Soon, Al's scream joined the chorus of the Lee sisters.

There at the end of the backyard, her flashlight illuminated a large group of waist high . . . *things*. Twisted and gnarled, the gray wrinkled creatures had elongated arms with long claws that almost touched the grass. The same claws that reached for them from under the bed. They were hairless, their faces almost reptilian as they stared with glowing green eyes toward the house. There must have been thirty, no, forty, of them there. Huddled as a terrifying albeit tiny force.

Everyone screamed as they rushed back through the open door into the house. But as they did, the hoard of demonic creatures let out an ear-piercing shriek of their own. A battle cry as they rushed out of the shadows and toward the back door at speed.

As they got nearer, they started to scramble over one another in a frantic, angry desperation. Clambering one over the other as desperate as they could and came barreling toward the house like a growing tsunami.

Back in the kitchen, Glen, Terry and Al turned, desperate to stop the tirade of twisted, terrifying things. Meanwhile, the Lee sisters were back to their ineffectual, constant screaming.

As Al pulled the door shut, with as much strength as she could manage, the things outside were nearly upon them, a wave of demons over six foot high, piled on top of each other, scrambling at them. She let out a yell through gritted teeth as she pulled the handle. The door was close to shutting, but the deformed things outside had significantly more strength than she had, and they grabbed on the door edges and pulled back.

The imbalance of strength moved the door open again as the demons' shrieks became more monstrous. Quickly, Terry and Glen each grabbed a part of the door and pulled on it along with Al.

With one almighty effort from them, the door slammed shut, and as it did, the shrieks outside immediately ceased, and the wave of monsters outside were gone. Only the backyard could be seen.

A strange, uncomfortable silence settled over the room, and the Lee sisters stopped screaming.

Everyone was petrified.

"Look!" Terry cried out as he pointed to the top of the door.

Wedged about a foot off from the top, a dark, scaly arm was caught in the frame. Putrid bloody gore oozed from within it and down the jamb. The arm wiggled as if trying to break free, but they could see outside. They could see that there was nothing on the opposite side to pull at it. No small demon on the frame, desperate to pull its arm free.

Then, as the arm moved back and forth, writing to free itself, a crunch of bone breaking and sinew snapping sounded. A sickly noise that made everyone grimace. After crunching some more, the arm broke free of the jamb and fell to the floor.

They all could only stare incredulously at the dismembered appendage as it did not stay still, it moved. It turned itself around by its fingers and raced back to the rubber edge of the door and somehow started to pull itself back through, even though there was only a paper-thin gap between this door and the frame. An impossible and surreal act as it quickly pulled itself outside and disappeared.

"Holy shit," Al uttered.

Terry stared through the glass, hoping for the arm to appear on the other side, yet it never did.

"What the hell's going on?" Stacy shouted.

"What were those things?" Patty added.

"The gate's still open, isn't it?" Glen asked rhetorically.

"I knew it," Terry grimaced. "We should have done that prayer thing more."

Glen closed his eyes. "We didn't close it," he said angrily to himself.

"Fuck this. I'm calling the cops," Al said, reaching for the kitchen phone on the wall. "They've got guns."

As her fingers touched the plastic of the phone, just as she was about to pick it up off the cradle, it started to ring.

Suddenly and loudly.

They all stared.

They had fallen for whatever was happening so many times now, Terry in bed, their parents in the driveway, monsters in the backyard . . . whatever this thing or these things were, they were going to great lengths to toy with them.

"It's gonna be those demons, right?" Glen asked.

"Maybe?" Terry answered. "You read that these things can drive you insane. Maybe this is how?"

The ringing was persistent.

"Ah, screw it," Al said, annoyed as she picked up the receiver, then spoke into it. "What do you want?" she asked with an attitude.

From the earpiece, a hollow ghostly static seeped outward.

"Who is it?" Stacy asked in a whisper, dreading the answer.

"Shh," Al replied, trying her best to listen. "It's just noise." After a moment, she spoke louder. "HELL-LO, ASS-HOLE!"

The static continued.

She shrugged. "I don't think that—"

An unearthly roar blasted out of the earpiece. So loud that Al had to hold the phone far away from her ear. Just as she did and the roar increased, the earpiece shattered outward.

Dropping the phone, she looked around at the dark house. Angry. "Fuck you," she shouted to no one. "Fuck allllll of you." She had reached the end of her patience with everything. "You think you can just come here and mess with us? Huh? Who the fuck do you think you are?"

"We *have* to close the gate," Terry said. "We have to go out there and do it right."

"You guys were *serious* about that hole?"

Glen looked at Terry, then to Al. "What did you think all this was?"

"I . . ." She really had no idea. Eventually, she shrugged. "Thought the house might be haunted? Probably? Or Agent Orange."

"In Toronto?" Terry asked.

Al shrugged.

Patty and Stacy were just lost in their fear and

confusion. "What is everyone talking about?" Patty asked her sister. Who just helplessly shook her head, equally confused.

"The pages!" Glen said. "They're in the other room. We need them."

The hallway from the kitchen was dark. Very dark. Almost too dark.

Glen shone his flashlight into the shadows. It barely did a thing to brighten the hallway. What was there was an unearthly blackness. A stubborn inky blanket.

The kids all looked at one another. None wanting to go anywhere that these beasts could be lying in wait. That is, not until Terry stepped forward, taking Glen's flashlight.

He took a deep breath in and fixed his gaze on the dark. "In the immortal words of Jesus Christ," he said, gritting his teeth, "fuck all those little asshole demons."

And with that, he sprinted at full pelt out of the kitchen straight into the darkness, with the torch held outward.

"Jesus said that?" Patty asked innocently.

"No, but he damn well shoulda." Al smirked. "Come on . . . Fuck all those little asshole demons," she said, grabbing Glen by the arm.

"Fuck 'em all," Glen repeated with a hopeful smile.

Pulling Glen with her, Al followed into the dark hallway, with Patty and Stacy racing after.

．．．

In the doorway of the dark living room, all five kids cautiously stood. Al and Terry both held flashlights, scanning the room ahead of them. It was a fraction lighter here than the hallway, due to the streetlights outside casting their dull orange glow through the shutter slats that still barricaded the windows.

They huddled close as they walked slowly in the room. Their sudden bravado took a backseat as they made sure nothing was hiding in here.

The house was still unnaturally quiet. Since the moans in the walls and the monsters outside had silenced, the quiet felt somehow thick and claustrophobic, like the whole house was being pressurized.

"Are you sure we can get rid of them with the pages?" Al asked.

"I guess," Terry replied, slowly looking at the table and sideboard for the pages. "They've got all these spells and prayers on 'em to banish the monsters. And if Tengler did raise 'em, he must have got rid of 'em somehow."

"What kind of monsters are they?" Stacy asked.

"You don't want to know," Glen replied as he turned to Terry. "Where did you leave them?"

"I thought they were on the table."

"But they didn't work last time you tried?" Al asked.

"No," Glen admitted. "But not like we got any other options."

"Aw, yeah," Terry exclaimed as his flashlight fell upon the pages scattered on the floor on the other opposite of the coffee table. "Wind must've blown them off."

"What wind?" Patty asked.

No one answered that, yet each thought the same thing, how were these pages on the floor?

Before getting any closer, Al held her hand up. "Hold on," she said as she crouched and shone the torch under the couch, checking nothing was beneath it. "It's clear."

Terry carefully stepped to where the pages fell and bent down to pick them up.

Glen moved his flashlight across the room. Across the vases and books, the framed pictures . . . then . . . then something grabbed his eye.

Stepping nearer to a bookshelf, Glen aimed the light at what should have been a familiar sight. A framed photo of the family taken last Fourth of July. An all happy, all smiling group shot. Mom, Dad, Al, Glen, and Angus. The Simon family.

But that is not what it was anymore. In the photo, each were in the same position as before, and each smiled the same smiles at the camera, but a grotesque change had taken place.

They were, each and every one, bloodily mutilated. Flesh ripped away, skin torn, eyeballs burst or dangling, guts dripping out, bone exposed. As if they had been mutilated by dozens of vicious mouths, who ate and tore and gored them, then placed them back in their positions. They impossibly stood, bodies and faces mangled, lacerated and maimed, smiling out of the image at Glen.

But he couldn't let himself react. He had cried and screamed and wailed at so many things that these monsters had done. He couldn't face more. He couldn't allow any more horror in. So, he averted his gaze and carried on scanning the room, not telling anyone else of what he saw.

"How the hell is this possible?" Terry said as he stared down at the pages in his hand. The *blank* pages in his hand.

"What is it?" Al asked.

As Terry flicked through them, his mouth lolled in shock. "They're all blank. How are they blank? That's impossible. This *isn't* possible." He then flicked back and forth through the pages with increasing alarm.

Finding another two pages on the floor, Al picked them up and saw that they were blank, too.

"I don't understand," Terry added.

But as she spoke, the pale, aged paper started to change. It began to darken and wither. As these pages dissolved in their grasp, they fell onto the floor as specks of filth. Terry wanted to scream, but he was too confused.

"Now what do we do?" Glen asked.

"It had all the answers," Terry said, his eyes stuck on the black flakes of pages at his feet.

"What about the bible?" Stacy asked nervously.

Terry snorted with a sarcastic laughter. "C'mon."

"There are prayers in the bible," Stacy added.

Patty nodded. "What about those priests? They get rid of demons, right? With the bible?"

Al considered what they were saying. "I guess that exorcist film did that."

Glen's eyes widened. "I remember something from one of the books I read at the library . . . It said that belief is key. Maybe you can't use any prayers unless you believe in them one-hundred-percent? It's why the spells we read didn't work. We didn't totally believe any of it."

"But, Jesus?" Terry sighed. "Really? These guys are older than the bible."

"Well, does anyone have a better idea?" Glen asked, looking around at the sea of blank faces. "Thought not. And maybe it's not about what you say but the belief in what you say."

"Okay, then who here believes in that stuff?" Al asked, getting a bible from off a nearby bookshelf. "It sure as shit can't be me."

"Or me," Terry agreed.

Everyone else was silent.

"Glen?" Al asked. "You believe in that stuff, right?"

He shrugged as he looked to the Lee sisters, who, despite how they acted, were very much believers.

"Okay, as you both believe in that stuff, what do

we read?" Al held out the bible to the sisters, who took it with a nervous smile.

"We'll find something," Patty replied as she opened the book for both of them to look into.

"We should've told Mom and Dad," Glen said.

Al smiled. "I kinda wish Mrs. Vandegrift was here. She's scared 'em all off." Seeing the worry on her brother's face, she stepped over to him "You okay, Houston?"

Glen shook his head. "Not really, you?"

"I'm scared, too," Al replied.

"And me three," Terry added. "I ain't got no shame in admitting I came close to pissin' my pants."

"This looks like a good place to start," Stacy said as he folded a page in half to mark it. "Our pastor always reads from Revelations when talking about banishing evil."

With a nod, Glen took the bible from the sister. "Okay, let's do this," he said, not sounding as brave as the words were intended to have sounded.

Standing at the back door, all five cautiously stared out into the dark backyard. It seemed peaceful again, but they all knew that meant nothing.

Al pressed her face against the glass, peering down at the bottom of the door, then to the left and the right, getting the best vantage point possible for each direction. There was not a demon in sight.

"Okay," she muttered under her breath as she

slowly placed her hand on the handle. "If those things rush again, we gotta be ready to run back here, okay?"

No one answered or even liked the possibility, but everyone understood.

The door opened easily and as it did, a breeze of chilly air blew in, and the pressure from the threatening storm was palpable. In the distance, the rumble of thunder broke through the otherwise silent night. A night that seemed *too* silent. The regular thrum of insects that normally permeated the backyard was absent. Now there was nothing. Just emptiness with occasional thunder.

"Where are they?" Al asked, looking around. "You think they just left?"

"Nah, bet they're waiting in the shadows," Terry replied.

"At least they'll only be the small ones, right?" Glen asked quietly. "Not something else?"

"If that book's right, if they *were* anything bigger, we'd be dead meat by now." Terry looked only slightly convinced by his words. "Then again, who knows how much of that is right. It had all that stuff about sacrifices. There's been none of that."

"Sacrifices?" Al asked.

Terry nodded. "It said something like the main big monsters needed two human sacrifices to be able to rule on Earth."

"Whoa, whoa, hold your damn horses a sec," Al said with a sudden realization. "Rule on Earth? Is this an end-of-the-world thing? As in an end to everything? *Everything*?"

"I dunno, just saying what we read." Terry then thought for a moment. "Well, it's what the handwriting in the book said. Tengler's notes, I think."

"You think? Terry, is this all from some handwriting in a library book?"

Al instantly became aware they could be out in the open for no good reason.

Glen spoke up. "The book had pictures of those little demons, the minion things. Exactly the same lookin'. And we can't just ignore everything that's happening."

"How do we know that everything in that book isn't actually making it worse?" Al said. "That thing you read out earlier could have been a spell to raise stuff. We don't know. You're both putting a lot of faith in some random handwriting."

"I'm not saying I believe the book, but what else is there?" Glen said. "What if it *is* the end of the world, and we can stop it?"

"And if we can't?" Al asked, keeping a watchful glance on her periphery, into the shadows at the end of the backyard.

"Then, at least we tried," Terry replied.

Ahead of them, the hole was still covered by the large panel of chipboard. Getting closer, they noticed that around the edges of the wood, a dull light filtered up from the larger hole beneath.

They all looked around warily. Unsure of what they were doing out there. Especially when whatever force was out here had tried to attack them twice.

They stood for a moment, staring down, dreading what this wood was hiding beneath it.

Then . . . a knock. A knock on the underside of the wood. Short, sharp, loud.

"Oh, fuck off," Terry exclaimed in disbelief.

Stacy turned to Al, wide-eyed. "What is *that*?"

"We should have stayed inside," Al added.

They stood, staring. No one was willing to move the wood, to see what was below, what was knocking to be let out.

The knock sounded again, this time slower and more menacing.

"What do we do?" Glen whispered to Al, who just looked back, confused.

The wooden board then shuddered.

Once, twice, three times.

Each longer than the last, trembling against the dirt around it.

Then the wood itself began to bulge inward, not cracking but stretching inward as if it were made of rubber.

With an almighty *boom*, the wood then snapped downward, splintering into two. The light from inside the hole shot upward as the broken chipboard fell in snapped shards. Deep, deep, down.

As they squinted from the sudden burst of incandescence, a strong wind was immediately sucked into the hole, pulling each of them closer to the lip. As all five looked down, fighting against the wind, they saw that the hole was a cavern of scarlet crystals throbbing and oozing like a crystal wound in the earth itself.

Before the wind could drag them in, they scrambled backward from the lip, but the gusts increased. Insistent and strong, not allowing them to escape.

"Grab onto anything!" Al shouted as the wind began to howl more forcefully around them. But there was nothing for anyone to hang onto. Nothing but grass at their feet, and that was not strong enough to take their weight. The winds pulled and pulled, dragging them nearer the deep, terrifying hole.

As they were dragged closer to the precipice, nearer to their demise, there was little they could do to stop it.

Then . . . the wind abruptly stopped.

Thrown into a sudden reverse, the gusts then blew out of the hole, like a long powerful exhalation. Pushing all five of them backward, off their feet and down onto the grass.

Through this gale that spewed from the hole, moans, wails and screams of beasts far below began to spill out. Furious and petrifying. As these monstrous noises sounded, the wind began to drag back in again. Inhaling. Pulling at them.

"Quick!" Al shouted as she got to her feet. "Read the bible!"

"I hope this works," Terry said, gripping his heels into the dirt.

"Me too," Glen muttered as he held the bible tight, unsteadily getting to his feet and opening it to the folded page.

The wind began to exhale from the hole again.

As he held himself against the gusts, with book in hand, the voices from far down seemed to recoil at its very presence.

Glen swallowed dryly. "Here goes nothing," he said as his eyes scanned the page. He had no idea where to start, so he started at the beginning. "D-Deliver me from my enemies, Father in heaven. Set me up . . . Set me on high from them that rise up against me. Deliver me from the workers on ini . . . iniquity. And save me from the devils of blood."

As he read, the voices came back louder. Renewed with greater rage and frustration. A fiercer gust of wind blasted out from the hole.

"I think it's working!" Terry said, with a look of relief.

Stacy and Patty both smiled, hopeful as they held each other.

"Keep going," Al prompted.

Glen nodded. "For, lo, they lie in wait for my soul. The impu . . . imp . . ."

"Impudent!" Stacy called out, knowing the verse well.

"The *impudent* gather themselves against me. They return at evening. They howl like a dog."

A tumultuous crack of thunder shook the whole house.

"But thou, O Lord, shall send them fleeing and destroy them. Thou shall bury the evil so they can walk the Earth no more . . . Because of thy strength, I will wait for thee, For God is my high tower."

The voices below as if that last phrase had the most power, suddenly quietened into soft moans. As they did, the wind relented as the light from the hole dulled in its brightness.

"Hey, it's working," Al said.

"I *knew* it," Stacy said, relieved.

"But I can still hear them down there," Terry added, not looking as happy as the others.

Glen looked confused at the book. "That's the end of the page. Do I just go to the next one? Stacy, Patty? Any idea?"

Stacy looked nervously at her sister, then to the backyard around them. "Let me do it," she said, unsure and nervous.

"Really?" Patty gasped.

The sisters were not identical in everything.

"I know this better than he does," Stacy replied, but her expression held less conviction than her words.

Before she could change her mind, she walked over to Glen. "Give me the book," she said, holding her hand out.

"You really don't have to," Glen replied.

"C'mon," she said with a sudden fear fueled

curtness. "It was *my* idea. You don't know what you are doing."

"Give her the book, Glen," Patty added, showing support.

"I'm sorry. I think I should do it. You haven't been very—"

Glen wanted to be nice, but with the amount of screaming and crying both sisters had done, he did not know if they should do anything except stay out of this.

Stacy grabbed the book off him with a yank. "Just give it to me."

Her fear came across as bullishness.

"Hey!" Terry shouted as he ran over and grabbed the book back from her hands. He was not intimidated by either of the Lee sisters. "You've been screaming since this started. Just go."

Stacy grabbed the bible back, but Terry had a firm grip.

"Don't be selfish," Stacy said.

"It's not a game," Terry retorted.

"Give it!"

"What the hell are you doing, Stacy?" Al shouted over, confused.

Terry then threw all his weight into pulling the book back, but as he did, his feet slipped as he over balanced. As Stacy pulled back, Terry then tipped over the lip of the hole and fell.

CHAPTER 8

THE STORM

Terry screamed as he fell, trying to grip onto the sides of the hole frantically. He fell more than a dozen feet before he managed to grasp onto what looked like a large red crystal but felt like warm, wet meat.

The voices beneath him, feeling his presence, gained a sudden strength as the thunder boomed in the sky overhead.

Terry stared down, and in the deepest recesses, through the light that shone upward, a shadowy movement could be seen. A shadow that was crawling nearer to him. He screamed as he closed his eyes, trying to block out the unreal reality he was in.

Glen, Al, and the Lee sisters stared down helplessly.

"Terry!" Glen screamed.

"Help me!" Terry cried back.

Stacy gasped as she dropped the bible, with a look

of shock and guilt plastered over her face she took a step back. "It wasn't my fault," she whimpered. "I was trying to help."

The wind picked up around them, from inside the hole and outside as an almighty lightning bolt filled the sky. It was the opening note for the torrents of rain that followed. The rain that finally released the storm's pressure over the town.

In the hole as the rain reached him, Terry gripped onto the fleshy handle for dear life as the shadowy things below got closer and closer.

"Please, help!" He desperately tried to climb up.

But the rain-slicked fleshy crystals crumbled and dissolved beneath his touch.

Without warning, the ground shifted. It moved in a violent motion as if breaking apart. Terry could only grip on, where, up in the backyard, the Lee sisters lost their balance as they fell to the grass and mud.

Glen and Al managed to keep their footing as they stared at the hole, whose contours were changing radically. Getting narrower. Closing.

"Hellllllp!" Terry screamed as loudly as he could, feeling the walls around him closing in as the things beneath him got nearer, and the demonic voices raged louder. "Someone read from the fucking book!"

Glen looked around the backyard in a panic. Frantically looking for something to throw down. "The treehouse!" he exclaimed as he raced from the hole, around the side of the house, to where all the remains of the treehouse had been piled up.

Al looked at Stacy, who was still on the ground with her sister. "Well? Read it!" she said, motioning to the bible.

But Stacy was in shock at everything, and Patty looked too nervous to help.

Moving as fast as he could, Glen grabbed the largest piece of wood he could find and dragged it back around.

When she saw him, Al turned to the Lee sisters. "If you're not gonna read, help me get more wood!" she barked at them, running to get more herself.

The hole was shuddering, the opening still narrowing. The ground around them in a frenzy as it juddered from side to side, all while the rain pelted down.

Glen, with the plank, put it into the hole, trying to brace its opening. As its mouth closed in, getting narrower, it soon hit the edges of the wood. The plank started to take the weight but began to splinter under the pressure, yet it stopped the hole closing for the moment.

"Get me outta here," Terry screamed as, below him, the dark things were nearly at his heels.

"Hey, I found this," Al exclaimed as she ran up with the old rope swing.

Without pausing, she grabbed one end of the rope and tossed the other end into the hole.

But Terry was farther down than she thought. The rope was not long enough.

The plank let out a loud, long cracking sound as

the hole heaved and trembled around it. The wood unable to hold it open much longer.

The Lee sisters then ran over with a triumphant look on their faces and a few two-foot pieces of wood in their hands.

Al was lying on the grass, trying to hold the rope lower down, but Terry was starting to slide deeper, as the crystals he was gripping with too wet from the rain. His hands frantically tried to grab onto a more stable piece, but everything here was soaking soft and membranous. He scrambled to get a foothold and kept reaching up to the rope with his free hand, but he was nowhere near.

Al leaned deeper into the hole, stretching to her limit. "Come on," she said through gritted teeth.

But it was no use.

The plank bracing the hole then splintered in half with a horrible crash. Pieces tumbled downward as only half stayed in place. Wedging the hole open for a bit longer, though half as narrow and much more precarious.

The largest broken part of the plank fell and collided with Terry's head with an almighty thud. Reeling, he only just managed to keep hold on the glistening, throbbing wall.

"Someone please read from the fucking book!" Al shouted as she did all she could to lower the rope.

Nervously, Stacy grabbed the bible from the soaking ground and frantically searched for a page.

Glen, peering down and trying to help Al, saw

what was coming up the closing hole toward Terry. Dozens of hideous arms, clawing out of the thick light shining upward, inches beneath Terry's feet.

"Deliver me from my enemies, Father in Heaven," Stacy finally read aloud, her voice trembling and terrified.

But no matter how weak her delivery was, the voices below could hear, and they roared in torment.

"Stop reading!" Terry screamed from below. The voices were almost deafening around him. "You're making them mad."

Up top, Stacy heard and obeyed.

Terry frantically reached up as high as he could, and with Al reaching down, the top of her body in as far as she could lean, the rope was only a few inches away.

But just as he was a few inches from salvation, damnation was only a few inches below as the demon claws swiped at his shoes.

As Al tried to lean further, desperate to reach him, she overextended. Her body started to slide over. She was powerless to stop it, as the rain having made the ground very slippery and muddy.

Seeing her, Glen jumped over and grabbed her by the legs, keeping her from falling. The rope moved down a fraction more.

Then what was left of the plank broke completely. The mouth of the hole free to continue to close.

With a final, desperate action, Terry pushed himself off the fleshy crystals and jumped up to the rope. His last chance. If he missed, he would fall straight down without another chance.

His hand managed to catch the frayed rope, and as it did, Al gasped loudly as she suddenly took all of Terry's weight. It was a good thing he was a spindly ten-year-old. If it were anyone bigger, she would have not been able to hold them.

"Help pull me back!" she shouted back to Glen, who immediately began to pull her legs.

Pressed to the limits of their strength and despite the pounding of rain from above, Glen and Al managed to quickly pull Terry out from the hole.

Above, the storm continued as the whole backyard was turning into a muddy swamp beneath their feet.

As Terry climbed out of the hole, he turned to Glen. "Start reading it! They hated it. It sounded as if it hurt them."

But both sisters did not hear him. They stared, paralyzed in terror, at the closing hole, out of which dozens of monstrous clawed hands started to emerge.

Glen raced over and grabbed the book from Stacy. She did not put up a fight. She just stared.

Terry, meanwhile, had grabbed a piece of wood and started batting at the demon hands. "Hurry!" he shouted to Glen.

Opening the book, Glen did all he could do. He started from the first page. "In the beginning, God created the heavens and the Earth."

From the hole, the voices shrieked as one of the claws grabbed Terry's plank and crushed it in its grip.

The Lee sisters covered their eyes and resumed their panicked screaming.

Glen looked at the book, then at the increasing fury of the monstrous hands reaching up to Al and Terry, who tried all they could to fight them away. With the wind and rain getting louder and heavier, he had a sudden flash of an idea. One he knew may be the dumbest he had ever had. But he had no other choice. He was out of options.

With a worried expression, he slammed the bible shut, walked up to the hole, and threw it down in it, between the attacking claws.

As the book spiraled deep down into the light within the hole, a sudden, magnificent flash of blackness exploded outward, knocking everyone back off their feet, slamming them down onto the muddy grass. The black beam shot up, replacing all beams of light.

The ground quaked as the thunder boomed louder and angrier and the rain fell down with even more power. So much so that the blanket of water coming down was almost impenetrable to see through.

The voices in the hole were no longer screaming in anger but in agony. Whimpers and yelps as a palpable sound of fear filled them as they whined and moaned. Their voices began to fade.

As they did, the quaking soon subsided, the

thunder got quieter, and the rain started to weaken until all it was, was a gentle mist.

Within moments, the five of them lay on the grass, drenched, muddy, looking around at each other.

Slowly picking himself up, Glen looked in shock at what was in front of him. "Uh, guys?"

The grass in front of him was smooth and unbroken.

The hole was gone.

Tentatively, he walked over to where the hole had just been. With his foot out, he tested it.

Terry, Al, and the Lee sisters also stood. All quiet and unsure of anything as they converged to where Glen was.

"It's gone, isn't it?" Glen asked with a hopeful smile.

Terry was not so sure. "How many times now has something just disappeared? Noises, monsters, visions . . . . And all of them return even worse? How do we know this isn't more fuckin' with our heads?"

Everything seemed normal and quiet, but each one of them knew that quiet could not be trusted. A lull before a storm was not reliable. They had no idea what this was or if it was over, but they all hoped.

Cautiously, the five kids walked from the backyard and into the kitchen. Soaked and caked in mud, they entered cautiously, Al leading the way.

"Hello?" Al called out into the dark house.

"Hello?" Terry repeated. "Any big scary demons there?"

"Or short stupid ones?" Glen added, feeling more relaxed and less scared.

They chuckled nervously as they crept silently through the kitchen and into the hallway. With no flashlights, both having been misplaced in the furor, they had no way of illuminating the darkness and just hoped for the best.

Finally, Al straightened up. "This is ridiculous, guys," she said loudly. "They're gone. It's over. The hole is closed."

With a confident stride, her footsteps echoed against the stillness of the house. Approaching the front door, just as she reached for the handle, a dark figure, tall and unnervingly silent, stepped out from the depths of the shadows.

It surged forward with speed, its elongated silhouette contorting as it moved. Before she could react, a hand shot out and grabbed around her arm, sending a jolt of terror coursing through her veins.

"Scared ya, didn't I?" Eric laughed as his goons, Stan and Guy, laughed from their hiding place up the stairs.

Switching the lights on, the whole house was immediately rescued from the darkness.

"Why didn't we try the lights?" Terry asked quietly.

Glen stared up at the bulbs shining brightly above them. "They all broke, didn't they."

Al slapped Eric on the chest, annoyed. "That's not funny, you ass."

Eric, noticing the state of everyone, laughed. "You guys been mud wrestlin' or something?"

Ignoring his comment, Al asked, "What are you doing here?"

Eric smiled as Stan and Guy came down the stairs, carrying a few six packs of beers. "We came to party, naturally," he said with a chuckle.

"W-We invited him earlier," Stacy added.

"Before all of this," Patty said. "Thought it would be fun to have a few drinks."

Al, with a dismissive shake of her head, walked over to the front door and opened it. "That's enough for one night." She looked at Eric. "Get out."

"Really?" Eric replied.

"Come on," Stacy said, sounding less nervous and more like her usual self. "We can celebrate winning."

"*Out!*" Al sternly repeated.

"Alexandra?" Patty said. "You can't just send him away."

"I meant *all* of you!" Al replied. "Out of my damn house."

Glen could not hide his smile.

"And it's Al, not Alexandra!" she added.

After grabbing their bags from upstairs, the Lee sisters left, dragging Eric, Stan and Guy with them. Despite the terror they had experienced and the monstrous things they had seen, both had reverted to their rude selves. The crying and screaming was now just an unspoken memory.

As the front door shut, Al closed her eyes for a moment, enjoying the silence.

"What are you doing?" Glen asked.

"More than the demons. More than the earthquakes. More than almost losing our damn lives." Al took a breath as she opened her eyes again. "The worst thing about tonight were those two screaming all the damn time."

"Yeah," Terry laughed. "Like we get it, okay, we're all about to die. Move on."

Having cleaned the mud off and changed out of their soaked clothes, the three of them were in Glen's bedroom.

Terry wore some of Glen's clothes. Ill-fitting yet at least clean. He was sitting on the bed, looking at the two halves of the geode. In the aftermath of what happened, his mind could not help reverting to Angus. What happened. What he did. What those things made him do. But he felt less guilt. Whatever happened was not his fault. He knew that.

Al and Glen, meanwhile, were busily cleaning up the broken glass from the floor. Al sweeping, Glen holding open the refuse bag.

"Mom and Dad are gonna be pissed when they see

all this." She sighed as she poured a dustpan of glass shards into the bag.

"What are we gonna tell them?" Glen asked.

Al shrugged. "Frisbee?"

"They won't buy that at all," he replied. "We *could* say someone broke into the house? We could have been out. Came back and found it like this. No idea what happened?"

"That's not too bad." Al smiled. "Don't try and explain. Be as much at a loss."

With the last of the glass in the refuse sack, Al took it from Glen and tied one end.

"It's gonna be dawn soon," she said. "Why don't we all get some sleep?"

"I can't sleep," Terry said with a weak smile, not taking his eyes off the rock.

Al had noticed Terry's sudden quietness after what happened and presumed it was most likely about Angus. "You know how you dug that hole?"

"Yeah?" Terry replied.

"And how you had no idea what would happen?"

"Sure."

"And how you cannot be to blame for any of it because it was *all* caused by those monsters. Angus was taken by *them*. Not you. The window was smashed by *them*."

Glen was staring at the broken window. "Why did they replace all the lightbulbs, fill in the hole, but not fix the window?"

"'Because they are assholes?" Al shrugged.

Terry put the geode down to one side and looked at them. "Can we watch some television?"

"Feel free," Al said, carrying the bag out of the room. "But I know what I'm doing . . . cleaning the rest of the mess up, then I'm crashing out."

"Al?" Glen said meekly.

"Yeah?" She turned from the doorway.

"Good night," he said softly with a smile.

"'Night, Houston." She winked as she left, closing the door behind her.

Having made their way down to the basement playroom, the old television had been turned on and played an old black-and-white movie in the background, its volume not loud enough to be understood but not low enough to be silent.

Glen was sitting, exhausted, on the rug with his back against the sofa. He could not believe any of what had happened. It felt like a distant dream. One that came and went fast. If it wasn't for Angus, the broken window, or the pile of muddy clothes in the upstairs laundry basket, he would have probably convinced himself that it was all just a harmless nightmare.

He kept going over what Terry had said. That this was not just about them or the backyard, but the whole world. Did they just stop humanity from being destroyed? Did the people in darkest Peru or on the African plains or the rice fields of China all owe them a debt of thanks to him for saving their lives? For throwing that old bible in the hole? That *really* saved the planet? Did they stop the apocalypse with a book bought years ago from a convenience store?

Meanwhile, Terry was not in as much deep thought. He was sitting on the sofa behind Glen, looking over the two halves of the geode once more.

"Well, the good news is," Terry said as his fingers traced over the rough surface of the rock, "we got a souvenir from all this."

Looking back, Glen held his hands out as Terry passed him the geode.

Looking over the halves himself, at the words carved into the edges, Glen quickly handed it back. "No offense to the demons, but I don't want it."

"Don't blame ya." Terry nodded. "It's all quite bad juju." He put the geode down on the sofa beside him.

The events of the evenings had been extreme, mentally and physically, and both felt it. As the television played its film, Glen and Terry watched silently. And as the minutes ticked over, their eyelids started to droop. Heavy and unavoidable, they both fell asleep.

The sound from the television drifted around the room like a low hum. The voices from the film were barely audible yet loud enough to quell the basement's silence, which neither boy wanted to hear.

But then there was something worse in the silence.

The familiar scraping noise coming from behind the television on the other side of the wall. It was only quiet at first, but it slowly grew louder.

Glen's eyes opened immediately at the sound, darting toward the far side of the room. His heartbeat picked up as he turned to Terry, who had woken up and stared with the same fearful expression.

"Gotta just be rats," Terry said, uneasy. "Right?"

The scraping quickly shifted, moving to the right, rounding the corner of the wall toward them.

Neither of the boys noticed as the television turned itself off. The soundtrack of the film disappeared beneath the scraping.

"Yeah, rats," Glen muttered in agreement.

But after the last forty-eight hours, he did not believe that. The book was right. Demons drive people mad. They kept acting as if they lost. As if they were beaten yet every time they come back.

As the noise crept closer, Glen knew it was deliberate. Not a hapless scurrying of rodent legs. Then, just as it got a few feet away, the sound of scraping stopped in its tracks.

"Rats," Terry said again. "Please, just let it be rats."

Glen quickly noticed the television had been turned off. He looked at Terry quizzically. "Did you turn—"

With an almighty rending crash, the wall beside them burst outward. Brick, plaster, and mortar cracked open as an immense skeletal arm broke through the wall. Clouds of dust and debris filled the air as neither boy could see the bony hand grasp at them until it was nearly able to grab them.

Reeling toward the middle of the room, Glen and Terry screamed as they watched the rest of the wall then break apart and a terrifying monstrosity emerged from inside.

The massive form tore free from the wall with a sound like meat slapping against stone. A grotesque skeleton, with cracked gray bones that hung with rancid strips of decayed flesh, dangling off it like tendrils. From its gouged open stomach, its entrails twisted and looped around its ribs, slopping outward. One end trailing to the floor and dragging bloodily behind it.

Its face, or what passed for it, was just a hollow remnant of a skull. The front of its head was gone, leaving a hollow chamber from the forehead to the top row of teeth. But the teeth themselves, as well as the jaw, were present and working as the creature bit at the air toward them. The sound it created was worse than the scraping, deep, guttural clicks and rattles, like a blizzard of brittle bones and flesh grinding together.

The stench it gave off was hot, putrid, and suffocating. The air itself shimmered in a brown-and-red haze as this miasma of death and rot staggered closer.

"The workman, he was real!" Glen muttered, aghast.

"I just made that up," Terry replied quietly.

The skeleton's head jerked unnaturally with a sickening crack left and right, flicking at each of the boys in terrifying turns. As it took a lumbering step forward, its partially fleshy foot left behind a dark and viscous footprint. Then it took another and another.

Terry whined a sound so small it might have gone unnoticed in the noise of the moment, but that thing had heard it clearly.

The monstrosity stopped, tilting its head with a grotesque curiosity as more of its guts dripped audibly onto the floor.

Then it moved, sudden and sharp, as if it had finally found its prey.

The entrails that hung from its rib cage then started to rise from the floor like putrid snakes. They coiled up and came to rest within the cavity in its head. Twisting around themselves until they resembled two eye sockets and a nose.

And as if on cue, over its mutilated corpse, whether on flesh or bone, small openings began to widen. Hundreds of tiny holes blossoming all over its torso. These holes were soon joined with two smaller openings above them. They were faces. Many, many small, screaming yet silent faces.

Terry and Glen both recognized what was standing before them from the book. This was The Demon Lord of Abominations.

Opening its jaw, the demon let out a moan that brought with it a gust of boiling, putrid air. This moan was a summoning as when it stopped, the whole room seemed to come alive with sound. From within all the walls, a multitude of screams and moans and wails started, along with a frenzy of renewed scratching.

"Run!" Glen shouted in panic as he made a break for the stairs.

Terry had no time to react as the demon bolted forward and loomed over him with a dizzying speed.

The demon's face then started to shift as it stared down. The intestines began swirling within the head's cavity like eels in a jar, slimy and wrapping over themselves until the guts started to protrude. And as they took up another form, it contorted the bone beneath it, and the creature's teeth buckled outward, forced into a new shape.

With a long fleshy snout and its teeth set in a new long and narrow jaw, the face had become a monstrously profane version of a dog, a nightmarish version of Angus.

The demon snarled loudly as it roared. Ready to attack.

"Terry!" Glen shouted helplessly from the stairs.

But there was no time to run. The demon lunged forward and enveloped Terry in not only its rotten and clawed hands, but his entrails broke apart from its canine appearance and flew at him, around him, wrapping him up.

The demon then launched off the floor and flew backward into the hole in the wall.

"No!" Glen screamed, taking a step off the

staircase to pursue. But he stopped in his tracks as the noises in the wall shifted to laughter and the whole of the basement floor unexpectedly dropped a few inches.

The concrete then began to heave, jolted down and up with force, throwing Glen to his knees as a network of cracks broke across it and chunks of stone broke outward.

Scrambling backward to the wooden staircase, Glen desperately stared back as the whole basement floor fell, cracking apart and into a huge abyss that opened wide. This was just like the hole from the garden but a much bigger, more terrifying one. The sofas, rugs, and television tumbled down into the void, with the hole quickly growing to the size of the entire room.

The staircase Glen clung to hung over the edge as he stared down into the vortex. But as he did, the wood beneath his feet cracked, and the whole step began to crumble away. Like it had been infected by a rot that quickly spread over it. A rot that soon moved up to the next step, then the next.

Not wanting to wait around any longer, Glen ran up the staircase as fast as he could as, beneath his feet, one by one, the steps crumbled away and plummeted into the hole.

Getting to the kitchen, he tore across the hallway and ran up to the bedrooms. Within the walls around him, the scraping sounds and monstrous cackles followed.

. . .

In her room, Al had intended to go to bed but, for the past fifteen minutes, had stared at her own reflection in the mirror. With all the jewelry and accessories gone, she stood in her jeans and a T-shirt, lost in thought. She just kept wondering who she really was. She wanted to be like everyone else but realized it was not her. Being like the Lee sisters was not her, and she sure wasn't fitting in with them mentally.

Slowly, she unbuttoned her jeans and started to take them off.

A sudden noise came from the hallway.

As she turned to the door, she did not notice the dark shadow creep from behind her, not in the room but within the mirror's reflection.

Up the stairs, Glen tumbled across the landing, tripping over himself and falling to the carpet. In a terrified rush, the fall hardly slowed him down as he got to his feet and continued toward Al's bedroom. From downstairs, the floor, ceiling, and walls continued to crack loudly as the voices and scratching continued.

"Al!" Glen shouted as he burst into her room.

With one foot still in her jeans, she looked up at him, confused. "What is it?"

She didn't need any explanation as the wails and scratching sounds raced into her room. And as they did, the whole house began to shudder violently as if a giant earthquake was hitting.

Glen couldn't hold his scream as he saw the reflection in her mirror, the dark shadows that quickly became clearer. With its entrails winding up to form the face in his empty skull and the many small screaming faces over his half-decayed body, there in the mirror, was the dark Lord of Abominations.

As the house shook even harder, the mirror behind Al exploded, and the Demon Lord stepped out into the bedroom. And with it, a cloud of putrid stench followed.

Al tried to run but tripped over her jeans and fell to the floor.

"Get up," Glen called to her.

The demon stomped closer as Al turned back and saw the sheer horror of the beast. A beast whose appearance was changing just for her.

The entrails furiously coiled inside the skull and made up a horrific fleshy shape of a female face. Its distorted guts gave this face extremely exaggerated features. It appeared as someone who was going through extreme puberty, with dozens of large pustules growing on the surface and bursting with pus.

The rest of the intestines then snaked over the demon's body. On its rancid chest, the intestines formed two long pendulous, sagging breasts, as between its legs, they formed the shape of a large phallus. One that seeped blood from its meaty tip and dripped down onto the floorboards.

Al froze, too scared to even scream as this thing approached. But as the sickly, rancid cloud reached her nostrils, she retched so hard that it broke her spell of terror.

With a frantic tug, she wrestled her leg out of her jeans and scurried toward the door, just inches ahead of the demon. Rushing toward the hallway, she latched onto Glen, dragging him along with her.

Turning, Al then grabbed the door handle to slam the door shut, but as she did, her gaze locked with the demon.

Inside, this monster's entire putrid body convulsed violently. The entrails that made up its face began to pulse until they slipped from the demon's skull cavity collapsed with a squelch, still attached to its guts.

Then, from the darkness, inside of the demon's skull, its body stood shaking, a small fleshy blob emerged. The throbbing mass expanded out of the skull, then dropped to the floor with a wet thud. As it splatted down, the blob kept growing and growing until two small clawed hands burst out of it and a minion demon was soon birthed. Leaving what was its embryonic sack at its feet.

Another birthing sack soon followed from inside the demon's skull. Then another. Then another. Faster and faster. And from inside each one, a new minion was born.

As the sacks kept coming and coming, the demon's body kept on convulsing as the flesh on its body began to decay and its bones became brittle and started to break down. With each new gelatinous sack produced, a part of the demon's body faded.

Al slammed the door to her bedroom and held it tight as she looked at Glen. "What the hell is that thing?" she shouted as the roars from behind the walls screamed around them, the plaster beginning to crack.

"It's . . . I don't know." Glen looked lost. He did not know how to explain what this was. He knew a name but nothing else.

"What do we do?" Al added.

"*I don't know*," he shouted, upset.

"Is there something we can read? A passage? Anything?"

Glen looked devastated as he spoke. "It took Terry." As he spoke the words, a look of horrified realization crossed his face. "He is the first sacrifice. The demon came up to get two. If he gets two, he can stay on Earth!"

Glen was about to cry. He had no idea what he could do to save his friend.

As the house still shook, the hellish voices sounded joyous in their anger as they screamed from every wall, floor, and ceiling.

"Dad's gun," Al commanded. "Go get it."

But Glen was stuck in his thoughts. "It's all my fault."

Then, from the thin gap under the bedroom door,

the slimy claws of the newborn minion demons started to break through, impossibly reaching through the tiny gap. They swiped blinding at Al and Glen's feet, probing, hoping to slash something.

"*Glen*!" Al shouted, pulling her brother out of his fearful depression. "Get Dad's gun, *now*."

"It's my fault," he repeated.

"You gotta stop that!" As Al spoke, she gripped the door handle tightly, trying her best to keep it shut but on the other side. "There's no time to be sad or afraid! I *need* you. Terry needs you. Now *go get the gun*."

Chapter 9

The End of the World

Glen raced down the hallway as, at a dizzying volume from every direction, the demonic screams shot at him. Every surface shook as the cracks that spread over them shifted and separated.

He had to focus just to keep balance.

Passing the banister, he could not help peering over the side, down to the ground floor, or what used to be the ground floor. At the bottom of the stairs, the whole room was breaking apart. The cracks that engulfed it collapsed as they fell into the vortex in the basement below. From the hole, which was growing exponentially and from up its sides, slimy monsters had begun to reach out. With only large serrated maws making up their faces, everything their talons could grab, they tore off and began to consume. Wood from the staircase, plaster from the walls, rugs, sideboards, anything these toothy monsters could grab, they then ate.

"Hurry!" Al screamed, frantically trying to keep the bedroom door closed from the battering demons on the other side.

Glen pushed himself away from this sight and ran over to the closet. Reaching its door, he flung it open and grabbed the long leather case from inside. With speed, he unzipped it and thrust his arm in, reaching to pull out the rifle.

But the case was empty. Feeling around, he reached in deeper but could only feel the leather interior of the case.

Just as he was about to yell his findings to Al, a piercing pain shot through his arm as something bit into him from within the case. Yanking his arm out, a small demon, about two feet long, clambered out, its mouth bursting with razor-sharp teeth, embedded into Glen's forearm.

This demon was not like the others. Its face was familiar yet horrifically distorted. It looked like Terry, complete with his mop of hair, but its black eyes bulged too big and its mouth stretched too wide. With its small reptilian body, it thrashed as Glen tried to swing it loose.

"Glen, hurry up!" Al screamed from down the hall as she gripped the handle as tight as she could, stomping on every demon hand that tried to reach out from underneath the door.

Glen yelped as he slammed the demon against the inside wall of the closet. But it did not relent its bite but just laughed through its muffled mouth as its claws reached out to rip at Glen's face.

Thrashing his arm around, Glen screamed as he slammed this diminutive nightmare against the opposite wall, then back into the shelves, but the thing stayed clamped down. Blood dripped out in thick red streams down his arm and seeped into his clothes.

Hearing her brother's pain, Al didn't hold on to the bedroom door any longer. Letting its handle go, she sprinted up the hallway toward the closet, trying to keep her balance as the walls reverberated around her, with the continuing chorus demonic cries as loud.

Before she could even get a few feet nearer to Glen, the bedroom door started to bow outward as the torrent of minion demons slammed into inside. The noise of their fury made her run that much faster.

Approaching the closet, Al lunged forward and grabbed the demon that had attached itself to Glen, but it was stuck into his forearm.

"Help," Glen whimpered as the tears fell down his cheeks, and the pain burned through his nerves.

Frantically searching around, Al looked into the

closet for anything that could help. A weapon. Something blunt. Something heavy. Anything.

On the middle shelf was her old Barbie's Dream House, and inside, she saw her once beloved Western Barbie Doll jammed inside one of the rooms. Reaching in, Al grabbed the doll from the house and immediately held it like a dagger.

"Get off him," she screamed as she turned and stabbed the demon's face with the doll's feet, puncturing one of its black bulging eyes on impact.

The monster howled in pain but kept its bite firmly gripped. Its small claws flailed wildly.

But Al was not giving up. She continued stabbing the doll's feet down onto the demon's head over and over. She then aimed its rubber feet down into the monstrous opposite eye. Bursting it on impact, she rammed the doll further into where the thing's brain should be. Desperately trying to force it to relent.

With a more angry than pained yelp, the demon had no choice but to finally let go.

It collapsed to the floor, still with the Barbie stuck in its eye socket and blindly clambered to the staircase. Hitting the wall before finding its way to the steps and casting itself off the edge, down into the expanding hole below.

Down the hall, Al's bedroom door finally broke outward as a wave of minion demons scurried out, falling over each other in their dozens.

Bleeding and feeling weak, Glen gasped as the horde of demons clawed down the hallway toward them. On instinct, he grabbed the closet door and pushed Al back inside and shut them both in, holding the flimsy door closed with his good arm.

"Hold your arm out," Al said in a hush as she watched the blood dripping from his wound to the floor. She quickly grabbed an old hand towel from one of the shelves and wrapped it around Glen's forearm. He winced in pain as she tightened it. Stemming the blood flow.

"You okay?" she asked.

Glen nodded unconvincingly, bracing for the demons to get to the closet door. Doing his best to ignore the pain. Ignore his tears. Ignore his fear.

"Didn't Terry say something about what would kill these?" Al asked. "When we were flying the rocket? I swear he said something. Something about a light . . ."

Glen shook his head. "I wasn't listening?"

"Think!"

But somewhere in his memory, Glen *did* know. He heard Terry say it a few times while they went over the pages that day. What was it? What was—

"Oh! It was that pure light bit. 'Power from pure love and light' or something."

"What does that mean?"

Glen didn't know and had no time to consider it as the minion demons arrived in their droves at the closet door. This multitude of beasts started pounding and mauling at its thin wood. Their growls and shrieks getting hungrier by the moment.

Seeing the long rifle case half open against the wall, Al reached inside.

"No, wait!" Glen panicked. Expecting another demon to come out.

Instead, she pulled out the rifle that had been in there all along. She then opened the front pocket of the case, bringing out a handful of bullets.

"But I looked in there," Glen said, confused, as he stared at the gun. "How is it there now?"

Al quickly loaded the gun. "We don't know what's real."

The tirade outside battered at the door as Glen held it closed, but his grip was weakening.

This closet was small, so small neither of them had much space to turn around. They could only stare forward at the door as it rattled with the force outside.

"What do we do?" Glen said.

"I guess we have to fight?" Al suggested, though her words lacked much conviction.

Neither of the siblings noticed as the shelves behind them were slowly consumed by a thick darkness. They did not see as the shadows extended and engulfed everything that had been stored here, leaving in its place, a large empty void.

They then did not see the presence stepping out from this void, not until they felt its breathing directly above them. A sickly, labored breathing that reeked of decay.

Al turned in a sudden panic and, without even flinching, aimed the rifle up to whatever was there.

It was The Demon Lord of Abominations standing where the shelves once were. Its entrail created face, taking on the form of large bulging eyes that looked down at her lasciviously.

Before Glen had time to see the monster that towered over them, Al pulled the trigger.

The sound rang out deafeningly through the closet. So loud both Al and Terry could feel it throughout every part of their bodies. Glen winced painfully as the sound hit him.

The bullet ripped upward into the demon's face. Wet matter sprayed out as the shot pierced through the intestinal face leering at her, but it did little to stop this thing.

The Demon Lord reached forward as its guts sprang into action. The entrails wrapped around Al as one of its large claws grabbed her by the waist, then pulled her back into the darkness with a violent yank while grabbing the rifle with its other claw and crushing it.

By the time the sound of the shot had abated and Glen could open his eyes again, Al was gone . . . taken by the demon. In the place of the darkness that it had taken her into, all that was left was the shelves, just as they had been.

Outside, the banging of the minions had also stopped, and the moaning voices and shaking walls had also abated.

Glen peered down at the floor and saw the broken remnants of the rifle as his body nervously trembled.

He was now alone. He was lost.

"No, no, no," he whined quietly. Still holding the door handle closed, even though nothing was trying to batter it down.

He glanced around the closet for anything he could use as a weapon now that Al was . . .

. . . *of course!*

There, on the shelf, was his birthday box from Al. *Big Bertha's box!*

Al must have put it back in here after taking it from his bedroom.

With his injured hand, Glen reached up to the shelf with the box on and pulled it down beside him. But something was wrong. The box was far too light. Peering inside, he quickly saw that all that was in there was some packing paper. The box was otherwise empty.

It must be in Al's room.

His arm began to throb with a burning sensation, but he had no time to do anything about it. The hand towel tied around the wound was beginning to become much sorer.

Though his flow of blood had been slowed, his thoughts were not.

His sister was gone, Terry gone. *The two sacrifices.*

Now what?

Now the Demon Lord of Abominations can rise and take over the house?

The town?

The country?

The world?

Summoning all his courage, Glen carefully opened the door to the closet and peered out into the hallway. The now destroyed hallway. With its walls, ceiling and floor littered with a multitude of cracks, the carpet torn upward, chunks of plaster broken outward and every surface being covered in tiny claw marks, the place was a wreck. Peering back at the front of the closet door, Glen saw that damage the minions had done to it. They had torn at the paintwork and wood to such a degree that they could have broken through in seconds had they continued for a moment longer.

The silence in this hallway felt as if it was filled with a pressure that made it uncomfortable to be in. Glen could feel it bearing down on him as he stepped down the hall to Al's bedroom door.

Inside, it was no less destroyed than the hallway. Everywhere and everything was cracked or broken apart.

Walking up to the bed, Glen cradled his injured arm as he got to his knees and peered under, hoping to see Big Bertha resting there, but all he could see was debris from the destruction.

He then turned his attention to Al's closet.

He knew better than to just open the closet blindly. He had no idea what could be waiting for him in there. Could be the small demons, could be the

Demon Lord, could be any countless monsters he had seen.

Carefully, he placed his ear against the wood. Hoping he would be able to hear if something was inside, but he heard nothing. Taking a deep breath, he grabbed the door handle. As he did, the house started to shake violently again as from all around the walls, the demon chorus of voices roared back again.

"Shut up!" Glen yelled, feeling the returned barrage of noise ripping at his mind. "*Shut up, shut up, shut up!*"

At the same time, outside, in the stormy skies, thunder boomed like cannon fire.

With a furious grunt, Glen threw open the closet door and braced himself for a possible onslaught of monsters to rush at him, but it was only shelves, upon which were piles of folded clothes, cartons, containers, as well as dozens of boxes. All neat and tidy. Everything labeled and in its place.

This neatness and order only lasted a few seconds until Glen tore into it. Pulling out clothes, tearing open boxes, casting everything aside as he searched each corner of the closet.

"I'll find this, and I'll beat you, you'll see," Glen seethed as he talked aloud, trying to convince himself to ignore his fear. "You can appear to me *right now, and* I'll show you. I'll show you all."

The shaking of the house then suddenly changed.

It was no longer shaking from its foundations but morphed into a rhythmic *BOOM, BOOM, BOOM* as what sounded like monstrous footsteps caused the whole building to tremble. And whatever it was walked down the hallway toward the bedroom.

Frantically, Glen reached up for more of the clothes and boxes, pulling them out.

BOOM, BOOM, BOOM. The steps were getting much closer. Slow and steady.

Pulling a pile of clothes, Glen couldn't see what was wrapped in one of the jumpers as it fell onto his foot, hitting with a sore thud.

And there it was . . . Big Bertha, on the floor. And beside it, the rocket's launching equipment.

His eyes lit up as he crouched and hurriedly fumbled with the wiring. Connecting the rocket to the battery as best as he could figure it.

BOOM, BOOM, BOOM. Closer in the hallway. Much closer.

Big Bertha was unlike any of the other model rockets Glen had fired before. He was not familiar with this system as he forced igniters haphazardly into its multiple engines, trying to get everything fit in their right places. Twisting wires together with his shaking hands as he just tried any formation the wires could take in order for the green launch light on the side of the rocket to illuminate, to show him that Big Bertha was ready to fire.

BOOM. BOOM. BOOM. BOOM . . . The steps came to a halt. Right in the cracked doorway. The Demon Lord of Abominations was here again.

Terrified, Glen turned the rocket outward as he

kept trying different wiring formations as time, but time had run out.

Unlike before, this demon's face was not in any particular form. Entrails from its open stomach swarmed around its body, fluttering in a fury, spraying its coating of blood and bile like liquid confetti. From its empty skull cavity shone a black void, spilling upwards. The darkness it extruded was impenetrable and seemed almost solid. Below this dark beam, its teeth chittered in short, sharp bursts. Between these, its long rancid black tongue shot out to lick the air as if it could taste the fear within the room.

This monster remained standing in the doorway as around it, the hoard of minion demons swarming inside.

The green light then lit up on Big Bertha.

Glen rushed out of the closet to get a clearer view and aimed the rocket at the demon, not realizing he had knocked one of the igniter wires loose, and the green light had flickered off again.

With a smile, he touched the igniter wire to the battery terminal, praying this would work. That this would beat this horror.

Nothing.

Looking down in a panic, he quickly noticed the green light was off, and the other end of the igniter wire had come loose.

But before he could reattach it, the minions were upon him.

Glen picked up the large rocket and swung it at

the beasts like a baseball bat, slamming a couple in the side of the head as the force sent them flying across the room.

Quickly, Glen reattached the wire, but before he could turn to the battery, one of the minion demons opened its mouth far wider than should be possible and swallowed it whole. The power for the launch was consumed.

The Demon Lord of Abominations then advanced, its tongue flicking toward Glen as its intestines flitted around. The hundreds of small, silently screaming faces within this beast's flesh and bone then began to sound. A chorus of terrifying cries. Some screamed for help, while some begged to be killed, some just wailed and shrieked in torment.

Glen stared at the monster coming at him and came to the realization that it was finally over. He had lost. He could not beat this thing. Throwing his hands up over his face, he screamed aloud as he waited for the end.

But those moments passed.

He was still sitting there. The screams all over the monster continued, but Glen had not been touched.

Peeking through his fingers, he saw that the demon and minions all backed away.

The Demon Lord was now less than six inches from Glen's face. On its haunches, it stared at him through the cavity in its head.

Through the dark light that spilled upward, deep

inside this blackness at the back of the skull, Glen could see the demon's face. Its true face.

There were two darker eyes that looked like a butterfly. Twin balls that looked like obsidian. Each of these orbs stared back at Glen as they shimmered with intelligence. Unblinking and indifferent, they held no emotion as they studied him.

Cocking its head, this demon seemed to regard Glen with the detached curiosity of a predator, having no need to rush but slowly sizing up its prey.

The screams that came from all over the demon's body then fell silent as the entrails stopped fluttering around its body, returning to rest within its open gut.

Glen could only stare back, pale and unable to react to the unearthly terror.

The demon then stood and stepped backward. Its gaze remained on Glen as it sidled back out of the door, followed by its small entourage.

In a stunned silence, Glen shook in fear as he was, once again, alone in the room.

A sudden loud noise from outside caught his attention. He slowly got to his feet and walked cautiously over to the window.

Outside, the hole from the basement had stretched out from under the house and across the full size of the lawn. It was only a matter of time before the house itself would lose its balance and fall into this red glimmering hellmouth.

The edges of the hole swarmed with demonic

shapes, clamoring their way out in droves and spilling into the surrounding neighborhood.

As the storm raged above, pelting the area with torrential rain, bursts of lightning briefly lit up the night. From Glen's vantage point, he could see many surrounding streets, and with each flash of lightning, the sight of thousands of demons advancing in every direction was chilling.

He finally realized that this was it. *This* was how the world was going to end. From this country, this town, this house, this backyard, because of him.

Looking behind, he saw Big Bertha still on the floor. Not knowing what he was planning or what he could even do, Glen picked it up under his good arm and made his way back through the rubble of the hallway and toward his own room, which had been left in no better state.

A thunderous clap of thunder shook everything around him as Glen had to hold himself upright against the wall.

Then a scream rang out from far below. A scream he recognized. It was Al.

"No!" he shouted in a sudden fear as he ran into his room and screamed at whatever could be listening. "Come back here! Come back here for *me*, goddammit!"

He paused, listening, hoping for a sign that the monster could hear him, but he did not hear anything aside from the storm outside. He then remembered Tengler's writing, that the summoner's only power over the demon is the summoning. That, a moment ago, he said the demon could come to him, and he would beat it, and the demon appeared. *He summoned it?*

"Where are you?" he began yelling with a renewed vigor. "I did this! I summoned you! It's because of me! So, come back here *now*! Take me instead. Leave my sister alone!"

The tears flowed once more as he got angrier and much more frustrated.

"What do you want? Blood? Is that it?" He took the hand towel off his injured arm and squeezed at the wound. Blood seeped out as he cried in agony. "Take me!" he screamed, the pain filling his inflections. "*Come back here!*"

But there was no answer, nor did he hear Al screaming anymore.

Glen then had a terrible thought. What if the monster who bit him, the one who looked like a twisted version of Terry *was* Terry. Could he have been turned to the dark side and made into a demon. Is that what the sacrifice is? Turning them into monsters? Is that what Al would become? And if so, will she come for him as Terry did?

Through the shattered doorway, a gust of wind drifted into the room. Not wind from the storm but from something else. The wind brought with it the familiar smell of decay that always followed the Demon Lord.

Then, the wind began to grow. Stronger and

stronger, it flurried into the room and became built to cyclonic blast as it whirled around Glen. The debris in his room began to pick up within it, spinning around him as he tried to figure out what was happening. Everything around the hole began to tremble.

Glen could see that, through the wind, the walls in his room were starting to bulge outward. The broken window frame cracking as it turned in on itself. The corners of the room were beginning to twist, the plaster crumbling yet staying in place. The whole geometry of the room was somehow shifting.

The demons must have heard me, Glen thought, *and are now coming to collect what I offered*. Scared, he climbed onto his bed and scrambled against the wall as he hugged Big Bertha close against his chest.

BOOM. BOOM. BOOM. The footsteps sounded again. The Demon Lord of Abominations was on his way back. *BOOM. BOOM. BOOM.* They moved as slowly and menacingly as before, marching closer down the hallway.

Glen turned his head to the wall, gritting his teeth for what was to come.

There, he saw it.

In the gap between his bed and the wall, the launcher he had bought for Al.

As if a fortuitous connection of events, Glen's eyes widened as he got up and pulled the bed away from the wall then dropped behind it, reaching for the launcher.

The Demon Lord of Abominations arrived in the

doorway, its body with hundreds of small faces over it, screamed in a terrifying symphony as its entrails were back to flittering around its body. Just as before, it entered the room, licking the air for fear. Behind it, the demon minions follow in a marching formation. This is what it wanted. Just like the book said. It wanted blood.

But as it stood there, Glen had already connected the launcher to Big Bertha and was now pointing the large rocket at the monster.

"I love you, Al," Glen muttered as he pushed the button without a second thought.

Just like the packaging had said: *No False Launches. Take Off Every Time.*

Big Bertha ignited. Exploding into motion, not giving any of the monsters time to react.

The rocket flew across the room with a hissing followed by a loud roar as it impacted the Demon Lord dead center, embedding into its open guts. The entrails that flittered around the beast reached to pull the rocket away.

The demon's mouth then made its first sound as it started to laugh loudly as its entrails began to wrap around the rocket.

Glen slumped down, thinking this had not worked.

But then Big Bertha made her grand entrance as the rocket then detonated inside the beast. As it exploded, a brilliant green phosphoric light filled the room. A light that got brighter and brighter, as its color then turned pure white, and the demon's laughs turned into screams of pain.

Glen covered his eyes, hiding in the gap between the wall and bed as the blinding white light from Big Bertha burst out through the demon's every orifice. Spewing out through every small screaming face over it, extinguishing the black light from its skull in an instant and then spreading its beam outward.

From the bedroom, the light grew and grew, and soon, it blasted through every room in the house. Through every crack in the walls, the white light shone through, smothering everything in its path.

One by one, bathed in the glare of the rocket, the minion demons started to shrivel up. Their flesh began splitting and drying as their bones cracked, and their bodies folded in on themselves. Their screams were short-lived as one by one they were crushed into dust.

For the Demon Lord of Abominations, the light that broke out of its body started to evaporate each part of its putrid, grotesque being.

Outside the house, the light from within broke outward like a powerful lighthouse as it covered all the horrors in its vicinity. The demons across the neighborhood were immediately caught in the glow and burned away into nothing until all that was left of each of them was a black gelatinous stain on the ground they had stood on.

From Glen's open window, like a crescendo to this unnatural cleansing light, Big Bertha let out a huge explosion of fireworks that cascaded out across the backyard in every color imaginable, then tumbled down onto the vortex beneath.

The dark storm had ceased its battle and started to clear, it, too, being pushed away by the light as in its wake sat a milky gray dawn.

This lasted no more than a dozen seconds . . . and when it was over, Glen's room was filled with smoke and stank of burnt, rotten meat. He could not hear the silence over the painful ringing in his ears as he slowly looked up from behind the bed.

The room was totally destroyed, his bedsheets scorched, and there, by his door, black sticky remnants of dozens of demons stained the floorboards and onto the hallway carpet.

Slowly standing, Glen carefully walked across his room, through the debris and into the hallway.

The carpet that remained in the hallway was almost soaked in black sludgy stains. There must have been hundreds of minions standing here. All waiting for the dark lord to take him.

Getting to the stairs, he peered over the banister, expecting to see the large beckoning hole, but that, too, was gone, along with the floor and furniture. All that was beneath him was dirt.

Then came a scratching from the closet behind him.

"Please, no more," Glen said weakly, unable to take any more horrors, gripping his head as he felt his sanity starting to fracture.

The sound continued.

"No, no, no," he whimpered as he backed away.

The closer door then started to open.

"Please." He pressed his back against the hallway wall.

But what emerged was neither monstrous nor grotesque. It was a furry creature with a joyful expression.

"Angus!" Glen cried out happily as he slumped to his knees, overwhelmed.

Padding out of the closet, wagging his tail, sure enough, it was Angus, who shuffled his way over and breathed his old dog breath, right into Glen's face. A smell Glen had missed.

As the closet door opened fully, Glen's face lit up.

There was Al, with Terry standing close behind. Where the shelves had been was a massive hole. Both of them looked terrible. Beaten, bruised, and exhausted. It was only Angus who looked normal and untouched.

Glen cried with relief, overwhelmed. The sorrow of believing he lost them, the grief of everything that followed, all melted away.

From the front of the Simon house, you would never have suspected that any extensive damage had been sustained on the inside.

Since they managed to get outside, the three kids had sat on the porch in relative silence, watching the day pass and the afternoon set in. The afternoon where Michael and Marcy Simon were due back from their holiday.

"What happened?" was the first thing Glen had asked in the hallway as he hugged Al and Terry but neither of them could bring themselves to answer.

The images in their head were simply too terrifying to put into words.

And they sat there, looking ragged and dazed, staring into space.

Glen could not believe that there were no screams from anywhere nearby. Didn't the demons get to destroy anyone else's house? Didn't anyone else see them? Maybe he had saved them all in time? Maybe Big Bertha did her work before the evil spread anywhere else? Whatever happened, the people they did see that day just walked or drove by with their usual content expressions.

Terry sat with one arm around Angus, patting him constantly. He still felt the grief and guilt of what had happened, even though Angus was really back, alive and well.

Angus, on the other hand, was more than happy to be sitting with them.

Al was the one who worried the most. Worried about what they could tell their parents. What could they possibly say to explain any of this? *Oh, hi, Mom. Hi, Dad. Terry and Glen raised some demons, and it ruined the house. But don't worry, Glen used a firework I stole in order to beat it. And Terry thought he murdered Angus. Now, how was your holiday?*

As they sat there, happy to be alive, happy to have survived, happy to have saved the world, Al turned to Terry. "You wanna make a move before our folks get back? You don't wanna be here for how mad they are gonna be?"

"Nah, it's good," he replied with a thankful smile. "If you both get in trouble, I'll be right there with you. We're a team, after all."

"Hell yeah, we are," Glen added. "The Demon Destroyers!"

"The Monster Mashers!" Terry chimed in with a chuckle.

But then, without any warning, a putrid stench of death broke through the crisp air, causing everyone to wince as it hit their nostrils.

"Ew, Angus farted!" Al exclaimed, leaning away and wafting the air with her hands.

The laughter that followed was half at the dog's wind and half in relief. The relief of pure, unfiltered joy that they'd made it through the night alive.

"No matter what happens with Mom and Dad," Al said, catching her breath, "let's just agree that we'll go with surprise. We have *no idea* what happened to the house."

"What about my arm?" Glen asked, holding up the evidence of their recent chaos, which was bandaged. "What shall I say happened with that?"

The group looked at each other, utterly stumped, before bursting into fresh laughter.

"We are *so* grounded," Al laughed.

"Ah, well." Glen shrugged. "I'm *already* grounded."

As the afternoon sun cast its glow over the houses, the three of them sat, a little bruised, a little battered but undefeated. Whatever came next, they'd face it the same way they faced the night. Together.

The Demon Destroyers, no, the *Monster Mashers*, were ready for whatever life threw at them next.

Even if it was just another fart from Angus.

The Mortal Tether
[EXTRACT]

by Nicholas Tengler

When one ventures into an act such as summoning, it is essential to understand that any connection forged between the summoner and the summoned is neither transient nor mutable. To draw forth an Ancient One or any of its ilk, whether through rite, incantation or sacrifice, is to create a tether that binds the entity not merely to the summoner's presence, but to their very soul. This bond is not severed even by the destruction of an Ancient One's manifested form; rather, it is rendered invisible, yet no less potent.

It is said that this tether persists beyond the grave, not only of the summoner but of the demon itself. Once called, a demon is forever tied to the mortal plane by the act of the initial ceremony, and no prayer nor exorcism can wholly undo this.

To summon a demon is to breach the barrier between the realms. This breach is akin to striking a hole in a dam. The act of calling forth the dark punctures a metaphysical barrier that separates our world from the realms of chaos. While this hole may be plugged, it is a repair, not a restoration.

To halt any inflow of demons may seem a victory in that moment, but the crack forever will remain. Over time, pressure will build from the other realm and with sufficient time or carelessness, this dam may shatter entirely, melding the two existences as one.

What, then, are the consequences of a rupture of this dam? The answer is both speculative and dire. Historical accounts suggest that such events, though rare, have occurred. For instance, the eruption of Mount Vesuvius in AD79 was accompanied by reports of strange lights in the sky. Some occultists suggested that the eruption was not merely a natural disaster, but the result of a catastrophic summoning, a theory supported by the mysterious disappearance of several occult practitioners in the region and the total annihilation of Pompeii.

I fervently hope that my writings will serve as a warning to any who would dabble in the dark arts as I have done. The summoning of Ancient Ones is not a harmless diversion nor a tool to be wielded lightly. I presumed it to be a boon to my world but instead, it destroyed it. It violates the natural order, an act of hubris that invites ruin.

Over the course of my investigations into the arcane, I have approached it with a scientist's mind, a lover's passion and a historian's rigor. My findings, though harrowing, are the culmination of years of not only study but devastating personal plight. I have lost so much, and now can see the truths of my world.

I hope you have read this book with an open mind as well as a cautious curiosity.

In closing, I shall leave you with the words of William Shakespeare as a warning of what will happen when (not if) the dam eventually falls: *Hell is empty, and all the devils are here.*

.

ECHO ON PUBLICATIONS

Official Novelizations
from Echo On Publication

In The Mouth of Madness

Night of The Comet

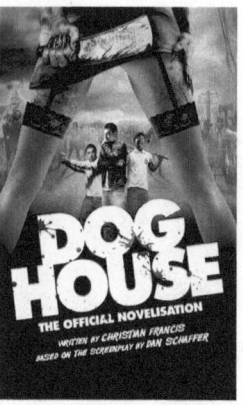

Doghouse

Witchboard

The Gate

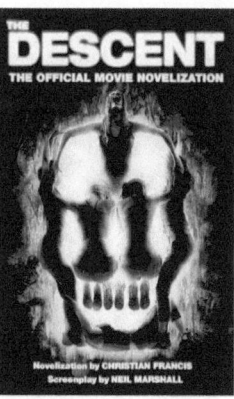

The Descent
*In Partnership with
Titan Books*

check echohorror.com for more details

Official Novelizations
from Echo On Publication

Beneath Perfectiion
(Tremors)

Session 9

The First Power

Maniac Cop 1,2 & 3
*Avaialble individually or as a
collected hardcover*

**Dee Snider's
Strangeland**

**3615 Code
Santa Claus**

check echohorror.com for more details

Official Novelizations
Coming soon

WRONG TURN

SHOPPING

WAXWORK

XTRO

THE DARK SIDE OF THE MOON

NIGHTWISH

SPOOKIES

·HOUSE·

FIDO

The MONSTER SQUAD

DRACULA 2000

Original Novels and Novellas
by Christian Francis

The Dead Woods
YA Horror

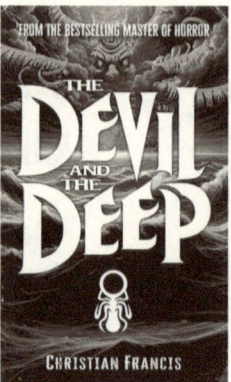

**The Devil
and The Deep**
Cosmic Horror

**The Sacrifice of
Anton Stacey**
Horror Novella

The Animus Chronicles Part 1
Everyday Monsters
Horror/Dark Fantasy

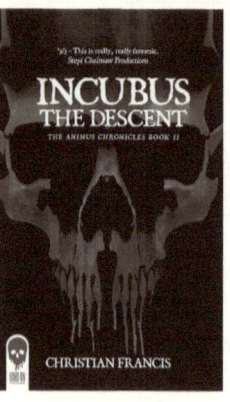

The Animus Chronicles Part 2
Incubus: The Descent
Horror/Dark Fantasy